Hard Landing

MacLarens of Fire Mountain
Contemporary

SHIRLEEN DAVIES

Book Two in the MacLarens of Fire Mountain Contemporary Series

Other Books by Shirleen Davies

Historical Western Romance Series

MacLarens of Fire Mountain

Tougher than the Rest, Book One
Faster than the Rest, Book Two
Harder than the Rest, Book Three
Stronger than the Rest, Book Four
Deadlier than the Rest, Book Five
Wilder than the Rest, Book Six

Redemption Mountain

Redemption's Edge, Book One
Wildfire Creek, Book Two
Sunrise Ridge, Book Three
Dixie Moon, Book Four
Survivor Pass, Book Five

MacLarens of Boundary Mountain

Colin's Quest, Book One,
Brodie's Gamble, Book Two, Releasing 2016

Contemporary Romance Series

MacLarens of Fire Mountain

Second Summer, Book One
Hard Landing, Book Two
One More Day, Book Three
All Your Nights, Book Four
Always Love You, Book Five
Hearts Don't Lie, Book Six
No Getting Over You, Book Seven
'Til the Sun Comes Up, Book Eight, Releasing 2016

Peregrine Bay

Reclaiming Love, Book One, A Novella
Our Kind of Love, Book Two

The best way to stay in touch is to subscribe to my newsletter. Go to

www.shirleendavies.com and subscribe in the box at the top of the right column that asks for your email. You'll be notified of new books before they are released, have chances to win great prizes, and receive other subscriber-only specials.

For permission requests, contact the publisher.

Avalanche Ranch Press, LLC
PO Box 12618
Prescott, AZ 86304

Hard Landing is a work of fiction. Names, characters, places, and incidents are either products of the author's imagination or used facetiously. Any resemblance to actual events, locales, or persons, living or dead, is wholly coincidental.

Cover artwork by The Killion Group

Book design and conversions by Joseph Murray at 3rdplanetpublishing.com

ISBN-10: 0989677397

ISBN-13: 978-0-9896773-9-4

Description

Hard Landing, Book Two in the MacLarens of Fire Mountain Contemporary Romance Series

Trey MacLaren is a confident, poised Navy pilot. He's focused, loyal, ethical, and a natural leader. He is also on his way to what he hopes will be a lasting relationship and marriage with fellow pilot, Jesse Evans.

Jesse has always been driven. Her graduation from the Naval Academy and acceptance into the pilot training program are all she thought she wanted—until she discovered love with Trey MacLaren . . .

Trey and Jesse's lives are filled with fast flying, friends, and the demands of their military careers. Lives each has settled into with a passion. At least until the day Trey receives a letter that could change his and Jesse's lives forever.

It's been over two years since Trey has seen the woman in Pensacola. Her unexpected letter stuns him and pushes Jesse into a tailspin from which she might not pull back.

Each must make a choice. Will the choice Trey makes cause him to lose Jesse forever? Will she follow her heart or her head as she fights for a chance to save the love she's found? Will their independent decisions collide, forcing them to give up on a life together?

Hard Landing **is the second book in the MacLarens of Fire Mountain Contemporary series—heartwarming stories of difficult choices, loyalty, and lasting romance. Watch for book three, One More Day, Cameron and Lainey's story, in the summer of 2014.**

Dedication

This book is dedicated to Richard, who continues to inspire and encourage me.

Acknowledgements

Thanks also to my editor, proofreader, Sue Hutchens, and all of my beta readers. Their insights and suggestions are greatly appreciated.

Finally, many thanks to my wonderful resources, including Diane Lebow, who has been a whiz at guiding my social media endeavors, my cover designer, idrewdesign, and Joseph Murray who is a whiz at formatting my books for both print and electronic versions.

Hard Landing

Hard Landing

Prologue

Pensacola, Florida

"You've got to get out sometime, MacLaren. Can't just hole up in this room all day and night, waiting to leave for Texas." Ryan "Reb" Cantrell, Trey MacLaren's roommate and best friend—since their initial days at the Naval Academy—was always up for a party. Trey took it easier. He was more discerning in his choice of both entertainment and women. They'd finished the basic pilot training program in Florida and now waited for transportation to advanced training in Texas.

"Thought I'd just hang out on the base, go to the club, and pack in early."

"Look, Cowboy," Reb said, using Trey's nickname, "we're leaving this gig in a few days and it's Saturday night—let's head into town, get rowdy, and have fun. It's time to p-a-r-t-y," Reb drawled in his pronounced southern accent.

Trey sat back and considered his friend's determination to get him out. Reb was probably right. A night away from the base, relaxing, might be good. Besides, he liked the city near the gulf.

An hour later, the two sat in an upscale bar near the water, eating dinner and sipping beers.

There was a small dance floor with a sign telling patrons a band would start at eight. It was a nice place. Lights on the deck were pointed toward the water, and the sound of the surf could be heard through the open back doors.

By eight-thirty, the place was starting to fill. Trey and Reb were on their third beers when a group of young women came bounding in, taking a table just feet away from the men and ordering a pitcher of margaritas. The music was going strong, with five or six couples on the floor and a few singles.

Every few minutes the table of six women would erupt into laughter. Trey watched, noting that they all were pretty—a couple of them truly stunning—especially one with long, dark brown hair that fell to her waist. Her eyes glistened as they traveled around the table from one friend to another. She was telling a story, using her hands, sometimes pushing up from her seat, then sitting back down to gesture with her hands again before everyone burst out laughing.

He wasn't sure what propelled him, but Trey found himself standing by her chair, offering his hand.

"Would you care to dance?" he asked.

She looked up, noting his uniform and confident air. Normally she stayed away from men in flight training, knowing they'd be gone within a year. They weren't part of the community, and would never embrace the panhandle life of Pensacola—her home.

"Sure," she answered, surprising herself.

"I'm Trey."

"Sydney," she responded, as they walked to the dance floor.

They danced one dance, then two, laughing and making small talk while they moved to the music. Reb was sitting at the lady's table, along with a couple of other men, when Trey returned Sydney to her chair.

"Take a seat, Trey." Reb reached behind him and grabbed one of the few available chairs. "These women are all from here and have been filling us in on the hot spots." Reb grinned as he took a sip of his beer.

Trey didn't want to dampen the mood by reminding his friend that they would be in Pensacola in just a few more days—why ruin a good buzz? He plopped himself into the chair and signaled for another beer.

An hour passed, then two. Trey wasn't sure how many drinks he'd had, which was unusual for a man who wasn't a big drinker. About midnight, the group moved from the bar to a large house on the water. Sydney told him it was owned by one of the girls—part of her recent divorce.

The party ramped up and continued at a fast pace, Trey never straying far from Sydney. A group of new arrivals joined the party, offering cocaine to everyone, which Trey, Reb, and most of the others, including Sydney, declined.

Trey led Sydney outside, grabbed a large towel, and walked onto the sand. He dropped her hand long enough to set down his bottle of beer and spread the towel out, then eased her down next to him.

"This is a beautiful place." Trey relaxed, pulled his knees up, and rested his arms on them. "Do you work around here?" Sydney had already told him she'd gone to school at Florida State, then returned to Pensacola.

"I'm a paralegal for a small firm in town. Great people, and the workload keeps me busy." She glanced his way, noting again his strong features, silky midnight-colored hair, and striking blue eyes. She'd felt her heart skip a beat when he'd first asked her to dance, causing Sydney to almost decline his invitation. Now, she was glad she'd accepted. Sydney couldn't recall the last time she'd enjoyed a night more. "Do you leave soon?"

He pursed his lips, for the first time wishing he had a few more days before his departure. "Any day now. Just waiting for transportation to Texas."

"Yeah, I know." She caught his surprised look. "All pilots leave for someplace else after a few months."

"You've watched a lot of them pass through Pensacola?" Trey didn't care if she'd dated one or two-hundred pilots—at least that's what he told himself.

Her laugh rang out, breaking the quiet night air. "Believe it or not, you're the first." She watched him tilt his head as his brows drew together. "This is my home. A part of life in Pensacola is knowing that new groups of pilots come and go all the time. Most never return. You learn early not to form friendships or get involved with any of them." She

4

took a sip of her drink and focused on the water in front of them.

He considered her words, understanding Sydney's need to be cautious and keep an emotional distance. Trey had accepted the reality of life as a Navy pilot when he'd put in for flight training, detaching himself from any emotional ties with the women he met. He finished his beer and stood, reaching out his hand to help Sydney up.

She started to pick up the towel but stopped when Trey set his hands on her shoulders and turned her to him. His clear, bright blue eyes darkened as his gaze held hers.

Trey brushed the back of his hand down her face and felt her lean into his touch. He moved strands of hair behind her ear, then ran his hands through her thick, long tresses, feeling the silky texture, and watching her light brown eyes as he lifted her face to his. Trey leaned down, touching his lips to hers—once, then twice—before capturing her mouth with his.

Sydney knew she should push away, stop this nonsense before she did something she'd regret. She wasn't a one-night stand person, and there was no doubt that this was a one-night stand man who held her. Attractive, smart, and funny, but a one-night stand all the same. Knowing this, she still leaned into him, running her hands up his arms, encircling his neck, holding him tight.

Trey shifted his mouth one way, then another, pulling Sydney close, and holding her to him with a strong hand on her back and one in her hair. Her soft moan encouraged him, and he began to explore her through her lightweight clothing.

She wanted this man with an intensity she'd never felt with anyone before. At twenty-five, she'd survived a broken engagement, and hadn't been with a man since. Tonight, she was ready to break all of her own rules.

He pulled back, searching her eyes, looking for an answer to his unspoken question.

"There are bedrooms upstairs," Sydney whispered, her voice ragged, lips swollen.

"You're sure this is what you want?"

"Yes, I'm sure."

Trey didn't wait any longer.

He wrapped Sydney's hand in his and let her lead him up the spiral staircase to a large bedroom at the back of the house. He pushed the door closed, gripped Sydney around the waist, and drew her to him, claiming her mouth once again.

Their movements were almost frantic as their hands glided over each other. Trey lifted her into his arms, never breaking the contact of his mouth on hers, and carried her to the bed. Within minutes they lay entangled in the humid night air.

He pulled away, reached for his slacks and removed a small packet. "Sydney, be certain on this. If you want me to stop, I will." It took all of Trey's effort to ask her again, but he needed to be sure.

"Yes, I want this, Trey." Sydney reached up and pulled him to her.

They continued through much of the night, then fell asleep to the sounds of the water lapping the shore.

Time passed, and before Trey knew it, light pierced through the openings in the wooden shutters. Sydney stayed sound asleep as Trey dressed. He looked down at her with a feeling of regret. A small smile curved his lips as he bent down to smooth back errant strands of her dark brown hair, and placed a kiss on her forehead.

He considered leaving a note, then thought better of it. They'd both known it was just one night. Trey took a deep breath, walked to the door, and looked back once more before closing the door behind him.

Chapter One

Kingsville, Texas
Fourteen months later

"Congratulations," the Admiral boomed out to the men and women seated before him. "You have earned the right to call yourselves Naval Aviators."

A burst of shouting and applause followed his statement. Later, the winging ceremony would be held at the Captain's Club. Orders to their individual fleet replacement squadrons would follow within a few days.

"Well, my man, we made it." Reb clapped Trey on the shoulder before turning to the third person who made up the three stooges, as he liked to refer to them. He grabbed Jesse in a bear hug and swung her around. She was one of two women to make it through and receive her wings of gold. Reb set her down as Trey slid past him to grab her.

"Congratulations, Jess." He leaned down to place a kiss on her cheek and wrap her in a hug. Few people knew that he and Jess had started to see each other over the last few months. Trey had always liked her, from the first moment they'd met at the Naval Academy years before. She'd grown into a stunning woman and one of the best pilots in the group. He was crazy about her.

Another good friend, Paul Henshaw, walked up and congratulated each of them.

"All right," Reb shouted. "To the club!"

Two hours later, each pilot had their wings, pictures had been taken, and they were free to celebrate in their own way. Some were married and headed home to party in private—others stayed on base or journeyed forty minutes to Corpus Christi to find a rowdy bar and enjoy their accomplishment. Reb joined the second group. Trey and Jesse opted for a nice restaurant and beautiful hotel room. Theirs would definitely be a private celebration.

******

Each of the four held orders in their hands—none had dared to open them. They hoped for assignments on the same base. Trey looked at Reb, then Paul, and finally Jesse.

"Ready?" he asked.

Each nodded. All three opened their orders and read the contents.

"California," Reb said.

"California," Jess smiled, then turned to Trey, her stomach tightening, praying she'd hear what she wanted.

Trey glanced at her, but there was no hint of a smile. His face was impassive. He looked back down at his orders. Her heart sank.

"California," he finally said and grinned.

"Damn you, MacLaren," Jess screamed before punching him in the arm and launching herself at him.

"Looks like we leave tomorrow." Reb turned to Paul, hoping he had the same orders. "So, where you headed?"

"California," Paul answered, his usual taciturn expression in place. Not one to show emotion, except for the occasional growl, which let everyone know something displeased him.

All four had been in the top of their class and all had requested the same base in California. They'd begin the nine-month training then be assigned to specific squadrons.

Reb turned to the others. "Guess we have to take this lazy ingrate with us," he joked, and slapped Paul on the back.

Three days later, they stood with the rest of the new arrivals at the large air base in central California. The four had chosen to rent a large home off base. The only rule—no pilot speak allowed. This was their place to unwind and live like normal people, not jacked-up fighter jocks.

Each had their own bedroom, although most nights Trey and Jess slept together. They hadn't spoken of anything permanent. Each still had several years' commitment to the Navy. Although it was clear they were devoted to and loved each other, their careers made marriage a hard choice.

"Where to this weekend?" Reb asked on a Friday morning as they drove to the base. The other nice aspect of sharing a house, besides sharing rent, was the ability to car-pool most days. Trey had always owned a big truck and couldn't imagine life without one.

"It's a three-day weekend, so I thought we'd fly to my family's ranch in Arizona. Unless, of course, you have other plans."

"We get to ride in the family jet?" Reb asked.

"Of course," Trey answered, as he concentrated on the traffic merging into the base entrance.

"I'm in," Paul said, then clamped his mouth shut.

The others in the truck just glanced at him. Those were the first words he'd spoken all day.

"Sounds good to me. When do we leave?" Reb finished the last of his to-go coffee and set the mug on the floor of the back seat.

"Robert Denton, our pilot, will be ready for us at three this afternoon. You won't need much, so pack light. Include boots."

******

Fire Mountain, Arizona

Reb had been to the ranch before and knew the drill. It wasn't too dissimilar from the Navy—early days and early nights—except they'd be modifying the schedule somewhat to include late nights.

Neither Jesse nor Paul had ever been able to visit, although both had received invitations. Heath MacLaren, Trey's father, picked them up from the airport at four-thirty.

"Hey, Dad." Trey dropped his bag and wrapped his father in a tight hug.

"Good to see you, Son." He turned to the others. "Reb, glad you could come." He shook hands with the young man he'd met once before.

"Jesse, Paul, this is my father, Heath MacLaren." Trey watched as everyone said their hellos, then loaded their gear into the large SUV Heath had borrowed from his brother, Jace.

"It's so good to meet both of you," Annie Sinclair, Trey's almost stepmother, greeted the newcomers as they walked through the front door. She'd also met Reb once before. Annie and Heath were to be married in six weeks and Trey had already made plans to fly back for the ceremony.

"Trey," Heath addressed the older of his two children, "show them where to bed down. Jace and Caroline have invited us over for supper—steak and ribs at six o'clock. Cocktails downstairs in twenty minutes."

Trey helped his father pour drinks and hand them out, emptying the contents of a large bag of bar mix into small bowls. He watched as Jesse and Annie made small talk. *Good*, he thought. It appeared like the two of them were hitting it off just fine.

"So you're all training in the same fighter jet," Heath summarized, after hearing about their assignments. "When do you learn which squadron you'll be in?"

"One more month and we'll complete the training. That's when they'll give us our orders." Reb accepted another beer from Trey.

"You all train together and live together." Heath sipped his Jameson and settled back into his oversized leather chair.

"And ride to and from the base together. Yep, lots of togetherness," Reb joked and put an arm around Paul, who shrugged it off.

Heath checked the time. "Guess it's time we get going."

Annie and he watched the four head out to the car. "I think something may be going on between Trey and Jesse," Annie commented.

Heath looked at her, surprised at the comment. "Why do you say that?"

"I guess it's the way they look at each other and follow the other's every move, plus a couple of small things that Jesse said. Anyway, I like her." Annie smiled up at Heath and accepted his quick kiss in return.

They pulled up to Jace MacLaren's house five minutes later. The two ranch homes weren't more than a mile apart. Caroline MacLaren opened the front door and strolled out. She hugged Annie and Heath, then turned toward Trey.

"It's about time you got back here for a visit," she scolded, while wrapping him in a warm embrace.

"It's a busy life, Aunt Caroline," Trey joked before turning toward his friends to make introductions. Just as he finished, a truck slid to a stop and a beautiful young woman jumped out, ran to Trey, and threw her arms around him.

"I wondered where you were today, squirt." Trey twirled his younger sister, Cassie, in a full circle. "This is my sister, Cassie. And I might add, she's off-limits to you two miscreants." He grinned at Reb and Paul, who'd taken an immediate interest. "Cassie, this is Ryan Cantrell, but we call him Reb. And this is Paul Henshaw."

"Hello Reb, Paul." Cassie offered her hand to each.

"And this is Jesse Evans. She's in training with us." Cassie didn't mistake the look on Trey's face when he introduced Jesse.

"Hello, Cassie. It's a pleasure," Jesse said as she reached out her hand.

"Same here, Jesse." She turned to Trey. "How long are you here?"

"Until Monday afternoon, then we fly back to California."

"Well then, I guess we best start making the most of it." Cassie laughed, grabbed her brother's hand, and pulled him into her uncle's large ranch home.

"Jace is out back at the barbeque. Why don't you men grab what you want to drink and go out to lend moral support," Caroline suggested, shifting her gaze to the women. "That'll give us time to catch up, without male interruptions." She smiled and started into the kitchen.

Jesse looked around at the massive area, with a high ceiling, that included the living room, dining room, and kitchen. She'd never been much for decorating, yet she couldn't help being impressed by the different textures and warm colors.

"What would you like to drink?" Cassie asked from her seat on a stool at the kitchen island.

Jesse walked up to stand beside her. "A soda would be great." She took a seat next to Trey's sister.

Cassie jumped down, grabbed a soda, popped the top, and handed it to Jesse. "So, tell me about you and Trey."

Jesse had just taken a swallow and almost spewed the soda onto the counter. "Uh, Trey and me?"

Cassie tilted her head and looked at Jesse, not saying a word, just waiting for her to fess up.

Jesse could see that Annie and Caroline had stopped what they were doing. They were as interested in her response as Cassie. She looked down at her soda, set it on the counter, and folded her hands.

"Okay, you've found us out. The man out there isn't really your brother." The three other women looked at each other, then back at Jesse. "He and I are alien clones, sent here to infiltrate the MacLaren ranch and infect all the cattle and horses." Jesse raised her eyes to the women, keeping her face impassive. "We're partners in crime. I'm sorry we didn't tell you right off."

Cassie burst into laughter, followed by Annie and Caroline. "That's the best response ever." She grinned and hugged Jesse. "You and Trey deserve each other."

Trey could hear the laughter as he walked through the patio door. "What's going on in here?" He stopped next to Jesse and put a hand on her shoulder.

"Jesse just told us about the two of you," Cassie said, hoping he'd take the bait, which he did.

He looked down at Jess, who avoided his gaze. "Well, we were going to tell you—just hadn't had a chance, right?" he asked Jesse as he took her hand in his, bent down, and gave her a quick kiss.

"Yes!" Cassie said and pumped her arm once in the air.

Jesse just stared at him, then burst out laughing as the others gaped at them.

"What?" Trey looked around, clearly baffled.

"Nothing, Trey," Annie responded. "We're just happy to see you two together." She turned her attention to Jesse. "And I hope you know we expect you at our wedding in six weeks. Assuming you can get the time off, of course."

Jesse dropped her eyes to their joined hands. Besides their two roommates and a few others at the base, the only other people who knew about them were the women in this room, and she assumed the men outside would learn of it—if Trey hadn't already told them. She had only her father and grandmother, no true understanding of the dynamics of a large family and how this type of life worked, but she'd like to try.

"I'd love to come, Annie. Thanks so much."

Trey squeezed her hand, aware of her struggle with including people in her life. She'd been considered somewhat of a loner until they'd gotten together. Now he could see her break out of her lifetime pattern and accept more people into her closed life. It all felt right.

Chapter Two

The following day, Cassie and Trey gathered the horses, and packed an enormous lunch before everyone set off for a long trail ride that would take them through a small portion of the ranch. Heath and Annie took the lead, with Jace and Caroline at the back. The others were spread out between, with Trey and Cassie moving between the riders, making sure everyone was doing all right.

Reb had ridden the last time he was at the ranch, and Trey knew Paul had experience from summers at his uncle's ranch in Montana. Jesse was the only one who'd never been on a horse, or around one, as far as Trey knew.

An hour into the ride, Heath pulled up to let everyone stretch and drink water.

"What do you think?" Cassie asked Jesse, who stood, stretching, already feeling muscles she didn't know could ache.

"It's beautiful out here. Trey talks about the land, how it goes on forever. It was hard to grasp how he felt, until now—it's breathtaking."

"Yes, it is. We all hope he'll decide to come back once his flying commitment is up." Cassie knew she'd be back working for one of the family companies after college. She wanted to share it with Trey, as well as her cousins Blake and Brett, when they were ready.

Jesse didn't respond. She knew Trey had talked about coming back, that he wanted her with him, but she just wasn't ready to make that decision. Ranching was as foreign to her as living in a crowded city was to Trey. Besides, her family, such as it was, still lived outside New Orleans. It was a place that held both good and bad memories for her, yet it was still her home.

Her daydreaming ended at the sound of loud, laughing voices. She walked closer to Reb, Paul, and Trey so she could make out what they were saying.

"All I'm telling you is to sink more into the saddle. You bouncing up and down like a pogo stick is about to make me crazy." Paul had said his peace and now took a long swallow from a bottle of water.

"I'll have you know, I took riding lessons at home and did quite well," Reb replied.

"Yeah, and when was that? When you were three?" Paul shot back.

"Five. But it's all right here." He pointed to his head. "Muscle memory."

Paul laughed. "Well, if you're relying on your gray matter, then at least I know where the problem is," he snorted and put the empty bottle back into his saddlebag.

Trey just stood by, listening. It was rare that Paul uttered more than a few words around people he didn't know well. He hardly spoke to the others in their training squadron, yet he was one of the best instinctive pilots Trey knew. The fact that he'd spoken this much with his family listening indicated his friend was relaxed and felt comfortable here.

"If you guys are through giving each other grief, it's time to head out," Heath called from his position atop his horse, Blackjack. He shifted his gaze to Annie. "You set?"

"I'm set," she replied and glanced to the others. "Looks like they're all ready."

"All right. Over the hill toward the Old Gulch and lunch," Heath's words drifted over the group as they ascended a rocky path to continue their ride.

The day progressed, ending with a tired group of riders collapsing in the large, great room at Heath's. Reb and Jesse spent considerable time in the hot tub, soaking their aching muscles after five hours in the saddle. Jockeying a thirty-two-thousand pound jet was one thing. Jockeying a flesh and blood, sixteen-hundred pound quarter horse was quite another.

After dinner, Trey loaded them into his dad's truck to show off the sights of Fire Mountain at night. The main area Reb and Paul were interested in was the old downtown. The courthouse stood in the center of a four-acre parcel, with businesses facing it from the streets on all four sides. At one time, during Trey's great-great-great-grandfather's day, there were more than twenty-five saloons and his family owned several of them. Ten remained, none owned by the MacLarens and all bearing different names than in the late eighteen-hundreds.

"We'll start here," Reb pointed, "move to each one, then decide which is best and finish our night there." He didn't wait, just pushed the swinging doors open and marched inside.

The other three shared a look. They'd been on these missions before—not one had turned out well for Reb. They followed him into the saloon, already knowing the night would be an adventure.

Each place had its own atmosphere, specialty drinks, music, and clientele. The first was a large western bar with dark wood, country music, and a good-sized supper crowd. They had one drink and moved on to the biker bar next door.

Old vinyl floors, dim lighting, a large beer and hard alcohol selection, and an aging juke box playing sixties and seventies rock and roll, welcomed them as they took seats at the varnished bar. It was much like an old bar they frequented close to the base.

Reb and Paul wandered to the back for a game of pool, while Trey and Jesse nursed their drinks.

"I'm glad you came," Trey said as he put an arm around Jesse's waist to pull her closer to him. He leaned over and nuzzled her neck.

"Fire Mountain is a beautiful place. Not anything like where I grew up." Jesse turned to place a kiss on his mouth, then straightened, staring into the mirror at the back of the bar. "Your family is great." She watched his reflection in the mirror.

"Yeah, they are. I'm lucky to have them. No matter what, I know I can count on them being there for me." He chuckled. "Even my squirt sister."

"You mean especially Cassie, don't you?"

"Guess she is pretty protective. Funny, as I recall I was the one protecting her while we were growing up. I guess times change."

"She worries about you—that much is clear. You're the only one not near the ranch, with a life outside of Fire Mountain."

"Except for my cousins up north, you're right." Trey sipped his drink and watched a group of bikers walk in and settle at a table against the wall. One uncle, Rafe MacLaren, Heath's middle brother, had taken his family and moved north to Colorado, finally settling in Montana a few years after Trey was born. He didn't know the whole story but knew a rift had developed between the brothers. No one had heard from Rafe in years.

There was also another group of MacLarens that lived in Nevada and northern California. He'd only met them once when several had traveled to Fire Mountain on their way to a cattle convention. Trey had hoped to connect with them while he was in California.

"She wants you to come home when your obligation is up."

He set his glass down and fixed his gaze on her image in the mirror before turning his eyes to hers. "And you? Could you live here, with me, after our flying obligation is over?"

Jesse stared back at the man she'd fallen in love with over the last year. It was never supposed to be this way. She'd had no intention of having a relationship with a fellow pilot or developing such strong feelings for someone else. Now that it had happened, she wasn't sure what to do about it.

"We both understand how tough being married to another pilot would be. Just look at Pete and Anita." The other female pilot in their training group in Texas had been assigned to the base in Virginia Beach, while her pilot husband, Pete, was with them in California. "I understand we could put in for the same duty station, but we both know there are no guarantees." She emptied her glass and set it on the bar.

"That didn't answer my question." Trey's eyes bore into hers now. He wanted to hear her commit—to him, to them, to some type of life together.

She was saved from answering when she saw Paul approach and take a stool next to hers.

"I swear that redneck was a pro pool player before he joined the Navy. Boy's got the damnedest instincts I ever saw."

Reb followed him, pocketing some bills and smiling at his opponent. "Don't take it so hard. You can get it back at the next place." He slugged down the rest of his beer and headed for the door before turning back. "Well, you guys coming?"

They ended the night at a small western bar with a loud band, college-aged crowd, and TV screens on every wall. The place was similar to the ones they'd frequented in Corpus Christi, packed with people lining up outside to enter. Country music blasted out onto the sidewalk, drawing more people inside. Trey often frequented the place when at home, and he knew most of the regulars.

"Hey, Trey," the bartender called and waved, between pouring drinks and filling beer mugs.

"How's it going, Charley?" Trey called back. "My friends—Reb, Paul, and Jesse." His gaze shifted to his friends. "This is Charley. He's been here since my dad started coming in."

"Good to meet you, folks. Doubt you can find a seat—pretty big crowd tonight." Charley nodded to a tall, slender, young man at the door. "Setup a table near the back."

"Sure thing."

"Follow him. He'll take care of you," Charley said and in an instant was back to the throngs of people requesting a drink.

"Guess it pays to know people," Jesse said and followed Trey to their table. No one seemed to mind that another table was being wedged in or that four newcomers took the seats.

"Pays to know someone in a small town country bar, that's for sure," Trey replied and took a stool against the wall.

No sooner had they ordered drinks than Reb and Paul took off, searching for fair game in the middle of the crowd. The band finished their set and the DJ filled in the break with lower decibel top forty country tunes. Trey wrapped an arm around Jesse's shoulders and watched the happenings around them. The crowd was his age. He wondered why he felt so much older and somewhat out of touch.

"You know, you still never answered my question," he whispered in her ear.

"About what?"

He leveled his gaze at her, knowing full well she knew what he was asking.

She'd switched to soda about two bars before and tipped the glass back for a long sip before setting it down and wrapping her hands around it. "I don't know, Trey. We still have a lot of years left. There's plenty of time to decide."

"That's not what I'm asking," Trey persisted.

Jesse looked into his eyes, knowing what he wanted to hear, yet not quite being able to say it. "I love you. Isn't that enough for now?"

He was silent for a long moment, considering her words. "Guess it'll have to be."

Chapter Three

Naval Air Station, California

They'd been back at the base a week. It had been a good—no, a great—trip. Everyone had enjoyed their time away and had already committed to inviting themselves back on their next long weekend. They got no argument from Trey's family.

The four had returned to their routine, finishing the training program before being assigned to their specific squadrons. The odds were slim that they'd all be assigned to the same carrier, but at least for the foreseeable future, they'd all still be flying out of California.

Heath and Annie's wedding was planned for the weekend after Trey expected to get his assignment. His plans were set. Robert would pick him up on Friday afternoon and he'd return to base on Sunday. The only question was whether Jesse would accompany him.

"So, what's for dinner, Reb?" Paul asked as he drove the four home on Friday afternoon. "Please tell me it's not more fried chicken and okra. You must know something other than that."

Reb's slow grin told Paul chicken was on the menu, again.

"Nothing for us tonight. I'm taking Jesse out to a new place I've heard about." Trey had his arm around her as they relaxed in the back seat.

"You are?" Jesse asked.

"Didn't I mention it?" Trey knew he hadn't, wanting it to be a surprise.

She tilted her head, narrowed her eyes, and gave him her 'you know darn well you didn't tell me' look.

"You'll like it. Trust me."

And she had—trusted him, and liked the restaurant, a lot.

"What's the name, again?" Jesse asked as she sipped her wine.

"Genovese's. It's owned by a cousin of one of the ground crew. He's talked about it for weeks and offered to make the reservation." He looked around. "Nice place."

"Yes, it is." She set down her wine glass to reach for the calamari Trey had ordered. He knew it was her favorite.

"Here you are." The waiter placed a plate of chicken marsala in front of Jesse. "And Osso Buco for the gentleman. "Anything else?"

"No, this is fine. Thanks." Trey smelled the wonderful aroma, picked up his knife and fork, and dug in.

It didn't take long for either of them to clean their plates. They passed on dessert but ordered an espresso for Trey and a cappuccino for Jesse. When the coffees arrived, Trey stirred his, deep in thought, clearly not focusing on the hot drink.

Jesse watched him a moment, wondering what it was that so fully captured his attention. She didn't ask, knowing he'd share it with her when the time was right.

He drove out of town to a small hill with a lookout that provided a stunning view of the valley below. Trey turned off the engine and sat back, enjoying the quiet. It was the one place that reminded him of home without being there.

"You haven't told me if you'll come to Dad and Annie's wedding."

Jesse wondered if that was what had been bothering him at the restaurant. She shifted toward him.

"I'd love to go, if that's what you want."

"It's not about what I want, Jesse. Do you want to join me?" Trey swiveled his head toward Jesse and his gaze locked onto hers.

"Yes, I'd like to go with you."

"Good." He was quiet for a long time before Jesse decided to break the silence.

"Is everything okay? You've been unusually quiet tonight. Is something bothering you?"

"Not really." He reached out and grabbed her hand. "I guess the last trip home solidified for me a question I've had for a few years."

"A question?"

"Whether I'd leave the Navy after my obligation is over and go home, or re-up. My time there, a few weeks ago, settled for me that no place will ever be home like Fire Mountain." He turned to Jesse. "That's where I belong long-term." Trey squeezed her hand, then let go. "I thought you

27

needed to know so there'd be no confusion about my plans."

Jesse thought about what he'd said. She knew her plans weren't firm. She loved to fly, relishing the adrenaline rush, the camaraderie she'd developed with the other pilots, and the structure. She'd made more friends in the last couple of years than she had her entire life. It would be a hard life to leave.

"All right," she said and swallowed the lump in her throat. "Are you asking me to make a decision now or just telling me your plans?"

"I'd never pressure you, Jess. You just need to know what I see as my future, and that it's on the ranch in Arizona. I'd like you with me, so yes, at some point you'll need to make a choice."

She let out a sigh of relief. "I can live with that." Jesse moved over, shifted so that she faced him, and wrapped her arms around his neck. "This is all new to me. I just need more time." She leaned down and placed a soft kiss on his lips.

Trey wrapped his arms around her, pulling her close and deepening the kiss. One hand crept up into her hair and held her steady as she opened for him, allowing their tongues to explore.

He adjusted her on his lap and unbuttoned her blouse, exposing her black, lace bra to his view. He let his mouth move down the soft column of her neck, then lower.

Jesse couldn't get close enough. She held his head tight to her, feeling the fire building, and squirming from the intense pleasure. She felt the cool air fan her skin when he unsnapped her pants and drew down the zipper.

"We've never made love in my truck," he whispered.

"Are you sure?" Her voice was thick, sultry.

"Oh yeah," Trey ground out as she moved her hand down the hard muscles of his stomach, then lower.

"Then I think it's time we do."

******

"Here you are," their commanding officer said as he passed out their squadron assignments. The pilots knew there couldn't be a bad placement. They'd either be on the USS Ronald Reagan or USS Carl Vinson, both with a home port at Coronado, California.

Reb was the first to read his orders. "Squadron eighty-six. The Reagan."

He was followed by Paul. "Squadron twenty-two. The Vinson."

Jesse read hers next. "Squadron twenty-two. The Vinson." She looked at Paul and smiled.

Trey was the last. "Squadron two. The Reagan." He was pleased with the assignment and the Reagan, but damn, he'd hoped Jess and he would be at least on the same ship, which would've made deployments easier to handle. His thoughts must have been evident as he looked over to see Jess at his side.

She rested her hand on his arm. "We'll deal with this." She dropped her hand. "Besides, we've made it. It's cause for celebration."

"That it is," Reb chimed in and clapped Trey on the shoulder.

"Looks like it's you and me, Outlaw." Paul came up beside Jesse.

"Outlaw?" Jesse looked perplexed.

"Didn't you get the memo? That's your call sign."

"Yeah," Reb said. "Something about Jesse James being an outlaw. Hence ..."

"That doesn't make much sense," Jesse protested.

"And who said it had to?" Paul understood her less than enthusiastic response.

Trey and Reb had been bestowed with their call signs weeks before—Cowboy for Trey. And as hard as everyone tried, no one could come up with anything more appropriate than Reb. So now it was official.

"So, what's yours?" Jesse stood toe-to-toe to the roommate who was now a squadron partner.

"Uh," Paul said as he scratched his head.

"Growler. What else?" Trey grinned and slapped his friend on the back.

Chapter Four

"Here's your mail." Reb handed Trey a stack of envelopes. "This is for Jesse."

"Thanks." Trey started sorting through it as he made his way upstairs to the bedroom he shared with Jesse.

It was only two days before Jesse and he would fly out to Arizona for his dad's wedding. He was ready for a change of scenery. The last few weeks had been brutal and he was ready for a break.

He pushed open the bedroom door and stopped. Jesse stood in a bra and panties, running her fingers through her short, damp hair. He never got tired of looking at her. She noticed him when he kicked the door closed and started toward her.

Jesse put her hands up. "Not now, Cowboy. I'm heading for drinks with some guys from the squadron."

"So you're cleaning up for other guys?"

She walked up and threw her arms around him before planting a kiss on his open mouth. "I'll be all yours when I get back."

He swatted her butt as he walked past to place their mail on the bed, deciding he'd sort through his later.

A few minutes later, Jesse checked herself in the mirror, grabbed her small shoulder bag, and dashed down the stairs.

"See you boys later," she called.

"Hey, wait up." Trey walked up, a cold beer in his hand, and leaned down to place a soft kiss on her neck before moving up to the sensitive spot behind her ear and finally to her lips. "Have fun." He turned and headed back to the kitchen, aware of the effect he'd had on her.

She stared after Trey, debating for just a moment before pushing the thought aside, of blowing off the squadron and staying home to attack him instead.

Jesse hadn't returned a couple of hours later, as Trey finished cleaning up the kitchen after his turn cooking dinner. It had been one of his dad's favorites—western chicken enchilada casserole. The guys devoured it. He slipped the towel onto a hook and dragged his body upstairs.

He had just pulled on a clean t-shirt, when he spotted the mail. Grabbing his stack, Trey sat back against the headboard, and sorted through it. A credit card statement, a couple of advertisements, a short note from a girl he had known in high school inviting him to a reunion, and an envelope from an address in Pensacola. He set everything else aside and opened the last piece of mail, counting two single-sided pages, plus a third paper with what appeared to be addresses and phone numbers, and a small photo that slid to the floor. He picked up the photo, staring into a small face and eyes that looked disturbingly like his.

Trey began reading, not comprehending at first, trying to wrap his brain around what the writer was saying. He stopped, then looked at the second page to read the signature—Sydney Powell. He couldn't place the name at first and let his mind play it over and over, until a light went off. Sydney, the girl he'd met just before transferring to the base in Texas.

His eyes went back to the first page and he started over. By the time he had finished, he'd broken out in a sweat, not believing what he'd read, but afraid it might be true.

Dear Trey,

Bet you never thought you'd hear from me again, but at this point, I have no choice but to send you this letter. I wish this could be done in person, but circumstances prevent it. A letter seems harsh, and that's not my intent.

We have a son. Trevor is fourteen-months old as I write this letter. He has your eyes and hair, and the biggest smile you could ever imagine. He is, quite simply, my heart.

I don't remember if I told you, but I'm a paralegal, or was, until recently. We were fortunate that I've been able to make good money and fit my schedule around Trevor's with the help of a good friend.

That's all changed. I was diagnosed several weeks ago with aggressive cancer. By the time I noticed any symptoms, it was already too late. The doctors have tried everything. They give me a few months, at most.

I found you through a Google search, or at least, your family. The receptionist at MacLaren Cattle told me you were stationed at a base in California, and from there I was able to find your address. Your name is on his birth certificate, and my attorney has your contact information. I'm sure you may be skeptical, and there is no issue getting a DNA test to confirm he is yours. My attorney is prepared to help with whatever you need.

I pray you will be able to take our son and give him the love he deserves. If not, I have a couple of friends who've offered to be his guardians. It's not my first choice, as I think he should be with his father, but only if you want him and can provide a stable home.

Contact information is enclosed. I hope to hear back from you soon.

Sydney Powell

Trey dropped the letter on the bed, staring at it as his mind raced over the implications of what he'd read. He paced to the sliding glass door that led out to a small balcony and pushed it aside, letting the cool, evening desert air wash over him. He walked out and rested his hands on the rail, taking several deep breaths before hanging his head and closing his eyes.

He wasn't sure how long he'd been outside, when he heard Jesse call his name as she entered their bedroom. Trey didn't turn toward her.

Jesse closed the door and looked around before noticing that the sliding door to the balcony was open. She started toward it, when she spotted the letter, open on the bed, and a picture lying beside it. She reached down and picked up the photo of a smiling little boy. Then she picked up the letter and saw it was addressed to Trey. Jesse stepped to the open door.

"Trey, are you all right?" He didn't answer. She looked at the letter in her hand. "Does it have anything to do with this?" She walked up and held it in front of him.

He didn't look at her when he answered. "Go ahead, read it."

Jesse read the letter, not wanting to accept what it said. "My, God." She placed a hand over her mouth, then fell silent.

Minutes passed and neither said a word. Jesse drew in a long breath and stepped closer to Trey.

"What are you going to do?"

He turned to look at her. "Call the attorney and get the details on a DNA test, then wait for the results. If Trevor proves to be my son, I'll fly out and get him, and bring him home to be with me."

"You'll bring him here?" Jesse was still processing the information. She knew her words sounded harsh, but the letter had not only impacted Trey—it affected her as well. They weren't engaged and hadn't committed to anything beyond their current living arrangement. She needed time to figure it all out.

Trey could see the confusion and disbelief on her face, knowing it didn't bode well for them. Jesse wasn't ready to commit to him, and that was without the prospect of an immediate family.

"This is where I live, Jess. Where else would I take him?" He walked past her, into the bedroom, then into the bathroom, anger replacing shock as her response sunk in.

Jesse could hear the shower. She sat on the edge of the bed and covered her face with both hands. There was no doubt she was in love with Trey. Besides the Navy, he was the best thing that had ever happened to her. She'd just gotten her first true duty station, just started on a career that would span at least a few more years. She fell back on the bed and hooked one arm over her eyes.

Trey stepped out of the bathroom to see Jesse on the bed. At least she hadn't run. He needed her here tonight, the feel of her next to him as he tried to assimilate the life-altering news in the letter. He walked to her side of the bed and turned off the light, then made his way around, pulled back the covers, and crawled in.

"Come on, Jess. Lay with me." He placed a hand on her leg and rocked it slightly. "We'll figure this out once I call the attorney tomorrow."

She stood, peeled off her clothes, then snuggled in next to Trey, wrapping an arm over his wide chest. "I do love you, Trey," she whispered.

"I love you too, Jess." He pulled her on top of him, cupped her face between both hands, then drew her down for a long, passion filled kiss.

She wrapped her hands in his hair, moving with him as he shifted his mouth over hers. His hands moved down her body, holding her to him as he lifted his hips to align with hers, letting her know what he needed.

Jess sat up, removed her sheer tank top, and let her body slide down his. She needed this night as much as Trey. A fleeting thought flashed over her as her lips moved over his taut stomach. This may be the last night for a while, where they could lose themselves in each other without living the changes they both knew were coming.

Chapter Five

Four days later, Trey was in the family plane, flying back to the base after his father's wedding. It had been a beautiful ceremony and Annie had been a stunning bride. He'd considered telling his dad of the letter from Sydney but thought better of it. Until he got the results of the DNA test, there was no point in bringing his family into it.

Trey had called the attorney at first light, the morning after he'd received Sydney's letter. It was seven o'clock in Pensacola, but her attorney picked up on the second ring.

"Mr. Egan, my name is Trey MacLaren. I'm calling about a letter I received from Sydney Powell."

"Yes, Mr. MacLaren. I'm glad you called. But first, I must ask, do you believe you could be Trevor's father?"

There was short pause. "Yes, sir, I believe it's possible."

"All right then. We don't know how much time Sydney has, although the doctors give her no more than a few months. Are you amenable to a DNA test?"

"Yes, sir. The sooner the better."

The attorney told him what to do, as well as the next steps if the test proved positive. Trey hung up, waited until the lab Mr. Egan had recommended opened, and made an appointment. After providing the lab with what was needed, he'd flown to his father's wedding, did the best he could to hide his anxiety, and flew home. All he could do was wait.

Trey watched the clouds pass by as Robert made his descent into the local airport. He reached for his wallet and pulled out the small photo of Trevor. Sydney was right—the boy's smile could melt the coldest of hearts. Fifteen minutes later, he thanked Robert, grabbed his bag, and walked down the stairs to the tarmac. He spotted Reb right away, but saw no sign of Jesse.

Trey walked up to his best friend, still scanning the area for any sign of Jesse. "Where is she?"

Reb jammed both hands in his pockets and looked at the ground. "She thought it would be better if I picked you up. She's struggling, Trey. Doesn't have a clue how to act or what to do."

"And she thinks I do?" He was angry. The test results weren't even back yet and she was already backing off, giving up on them.

"Give her time, man. She went for a run with some of the guys from her squadron. Should be home by the time we get there."

Trey threw his bag into the back of Reb's truck and climbed in. Anger worked its way up his body, until he could no longer contain his thoughts. "Shit. What a mess."

"That it is, but it will work out. No matter what, you're stuck with Growler and me. Hey, remember that movie, *Three Men and a Baby*?"

Trey scrubbed his hands over his face. "Ah, shit," he repeated, and sat back for the short trip home.

******

He'd showered, stowed his gear, then plopped in front of the television, watching some unimportant baseball game and listening to Reb and Paul argue over whose turn it was to clean the oven. Trey looked at his cell. No message or text from Jesse. He heard the front door open and swung his eyes toward it.

Jesse walked in, followed by two others—men he recognized from their training time at the base. He stood, shook hands with them, and started to pull Jesse into a hug when she stepped back. The men looked at the floor before walking around Trey to find Reb and Paul.

"What's going on, Jess?" His heart was in his throat, his mind fogged by what he knew was coming.

"Let's talk upstairs." She turned toward the stairs leading to their bedroom.

Once inside, Trey closed the door, folded his arms over his chest, and leaned his shoulder against the wall. "So, tell me what's in your head right now."

"I think it's best if I move out."

Trey didn't respond, he couldn't. He stared at a woman he thought he knew, and loved, and she'd just told him their relationship meant nothing to her.

Jesse walked up to him and placed her hands on his folded arms. He pulled away.

"Look, Trey. From the picture, we both know what the test results will show. You'll need to fly out and bring your son back here. That's good, and right, and as it should be. But I shouldn't be here. He's going to lose his mother, and have a father he doesn't know. You and I..." she signaled with her hands between the two of them, "well, we don't know yet where we're going. Believe me, it's not right to have me here, letting him think I'm his new mother, when that may not be the case. It's not fair to him."

His jaw tightened and he leveled his gaze at her. "Or to you."

Jesse recoiled at the implied accusation, but what could she say? He was partially right. "We don't have to stop seeing each other. Things can go on as they were, we just won't be living together." Her heart thudded in her chest at the look Trey gave her. She knew he was already shutting her out. She loved him, didn't want to lose him, but she wasn't ready to help raise a child.

Trey pushed from the wall and walked to the dresser. He opened a small case on top, took out a key, and handed it to Jesse.

"What's this?"

"The extra key to your Jeep. I'm guessing you'll be giving it to one of the two men downstairs." He stepped back and turned toward the door, then swung his hardened gaze back to Jesse. "Goodbye, Jesse. Fly safe." Trey shut the door behind him.

"Trey, wait..." she began, but it was too late. Jesse stood, frozen in place, not expecting him to react this way. She had thought he'd understand, agree that it was the best thing for him and his son, at least for a while. The boy would need stability, something she knew Trey could provide.

Jesse hadn't expected Trey to just let her go, not even listen to her reasons. She thought he'd know she still wanted him, loved him. That wasn't the case. She'd misjudged his reaction and mishandled the approach. He'd cut her out.

Jesse heard Trey's truck start, heard the wheels screech as he pulled away. Her heart squeezed. Tears burned her eyes, but she refused to let them fall.

Minutes passed. The room was so quiet she could hear the small clock ticking next to her side of their bed—his bed now. Jesse finally turned to grab her two suitcases and duffle from the closet. It took no more than twenty minutes to pack everything. She looked around. Trey had bought all the furniture. Her eyes stopped on a small jewelry box he'd given her last Christmas. She opened it to see the ring, pendant, and earrings he'd placed inside for Valentine's Day. There was also a picture of the two of them in their flight suits, laughing at a joke Reb had made. She debated only a moment before opening her duffle and placing the box inside.

She walked down the stairs with the two suitcases and the duffle flung over her shoulder.

"I'll get that," Paul said and took the suitcases from her. Her new roommates were outside, talking with Reb, looking as if they felt as awkward as the rest of them. The truth was, at this point, most everyone at the base knew Trey and Jesse were a couple, had been for some time. One of her new roommates was in the same squadron as Trey. Her decision had now impacted more than just Trey and her. She cringed at what a bad situation she'd created.

"You sure about his, Jesse?" Paul asked as he set down her bags next to her car. "You can end this nonsense right now. Let me take the bags back inside."

She shook her head. "No. I'm afraid I've really botched it this time. You should have seen the look in his eyes." Jesse licked her lips and worked to stem the tears she felt. She refused to give in to them. Not her. Not a Naval Aviator. She'd made her decision and now she had to live with it.

Paul stared down at her, seeing the pain and regret, not knowing what to say to change her mind. "If that's what you want, Outlaw," he said, using her call sign. "I'll see you in the morning. You know where to find me." He glanced at the house in time to see Reb walk out with her two new roommates.

They carried a few small items that belonged to Jesse—a pine bookcase, a few pictures, some dishes, and a box of books. Reb had taken care of it all, while she'd been upstairs, trying to gain the courage to go through with her decision.

"That's all of it." Reb looked at her and realized he didn't know what to say. What he did know was that she was making a huge mistake, but it was hers to make. "See you on base." He didn't try to hug her. Somehow he knew it would feel false.

"Yeah. See you on base." Jesse got in her Jeep, pulled out of the driveway, and drove to her new home a few blocks away. It occurred to her that she wasn't leaving just Trey behind. She was leaving what had become her family, the only people who had truly accepted her the way she was, who made no demands, and expected little, except for her friendship and loyalty. Jesse felt as if she'd let them all down.

******

Thirty-six hours later, Trey held the results of the DNA paternity test in his hand. Positive. He'd really had no doubt. It was a formality that he felt needed to be done to move forward.

Trey made an appointment with his commander, obtained approval for a two-week emergency leave, then called his father to see about using the family plane. That was the toughest call of all.

As he'd expected, his dad and Annie were one-hundred percent behind him. No questions, just asking what they could do and when they could meet their first grandson.

Heath scheduled the plane to take Trey to Pensacola, then bring him and Trevor back to Fire

Mountain. They'd spend a few days on the ranch, then fly back to California in time for them to get settled before Trey had to report back to the base. His dad and Annie's reactions were the total opposite of Jesse's. The sense of relief he felt was enormous.

He hadn't seen or heard from Jesse since she'd bailed. Neither Reb nor Paul dared to mention her name, and all pictures that included her had disappeared. The three spent a couple of nights before Trey flew out to Florida, buying kid's furniture, toys, clothes, and converting the office they'd all shared into a place where any little boy would feel at home. By the time Friday morning arrived, they were ready for their newest roommate.

"We're staying in Pensacola until you're ready to fly back," Robert told him on their approach to the local airport. He and the co-pilot, Todd Franks, had worked for MacLaren Cattle for years. "Heath scheduled a car for you. Todd and I have our own. Keep us posted." Robert shook Trey's hand before he headed toward the rental car.

Thirty minutes later, Trey stood outside Mr. Egan's office, straightening his uniform, and settling his hat on his head. He wasn't sure why, he knew it would come off within seconds of walking into the office. He reached for the handle and pushed the door open.

An older woman with graying hair sat behind the desk, typing on a computer keyboard, while simultaneously listening to a caller on the phone.

"Yes, sir, I have it. Don't worry, it will all be taken care of." She hung up the phone and looked to the gentleman who stood before her. "You must be Lieutenant MacLaren."

"Yes, ma'am." He took off his hat and stood erect.

"Well, you're every bit as handsome as Sydney said."

Trey just stared, surprised that Sydney remembered much about him. He still held a vague image of her laughing, her long brown hair rustling in the ocean breeze, her passion filled eyes gazing up into his. The memory caused a strange aching sensation.

"Well, sit down and relax. Mr. Egan will be here in twenty minutes. He got delayed behind some tractor-trailer wreck on the interstate. Coffee?"

"No, ma'am." Trey swallowed hard, trying to control the small tremor that shook his body. How was it he could drive a high-powered jet, yet get all jacked up over one fourteen-month-old little boy? His foot started tapping on the floor, and he fidgeted with the brim of his hat. He had to get control of himself.

"All right, Lieutenant, that's enough."

"Ma'am?"

"You look like you're ready to jump out of your skin. I understand this is tough, but you are doing the right thing. My son flies out of Oceana. You give him big planes and speed all day long and he doesn't flinch. But if his four-year-old daughter bursts into tears over something, he's a wreck."

She shook her head. "So, I have coffee, soda, whiskey, and scotch. Which will it be?"

Trey smiled for the first time in a few days. "Whiskey, ma'am, and water, please."

She walked to the back, then reappeared a few minutes later. "Here you go. Let me know if one isn't enough."

Chapter Six

Trey looked up as the door burst open and a round, older man hurried up to stand in front of him. "You must be Lieutenant MacLaren. I'm Oliver Egan." The man extended his hand. "Apologies for keeping you waiting. I assume my wife took care of you?"

Trey stood and accepted the offered hand. "Yes, sir, she sure did." He cast an eye at Mrs. Egan, who winked in reply.

"Good. Follow me and we'll get this going." Egan strode into his office, moved stacks of paper around, and placed his briefcase on his desk. Opening it, he rummaged around before finding what he sought. "Here it is." He held up a set of documents, then sat down.

"Mr. Egan, how is Sydney doing?" Trey asked, not wanting to push, but needing to understand the situation.

Egan lifted his gaze and removed his glasses. "Not well, I'm afraid. She's on pain killers, and as I'm sure you can imagine, groggy most of the time." He let out a sigh. "It's such a shame. She is one of the finest young women I know. Worked for me, up until it became clear she couldn't handle the job. I've kept her on full pay, and she does have medical insurance, so she's not expecting any help with that."

Trey cleared his throat. "I'm not as concerned with the medical expenses as much as I am about her getting the best treatment. There's nothing that can be done?"

"Unfortunately not. It is a very aggressive, rare form of cancer. My understanding is that it would have had to be diagnosed very early for her to have any chance of recovery. The odds were against her from the start." He leveled his gaze at Trey. "Are you sure you want to take on the responsibility of raising your son? It's a big challenge for a single officer."

Trey didn't hesitate. "Yes, sir. Trevor is my son, and he'll live with me." He returned the attorney's stare. "He won't want for love, family, or opportunity. I can assure you of that."

Egan sat back. "That's good to hear, as I know Sydney has been concerned about springing all this on you without warning."

"I don't understand why she didn't get in touch with me when she learned she was pregnant. I would have helped with Trevor all along." This was the question that had haunted him since he'd received Sydney's letter.

"You must understand, Sydney is a stubborn, independent young lady. She came right out and told Mrs. Egan and I that it was a one night thing, no commitments, and she was determined not to burden you with it."

"Burden? Having my own son would not have been a burden, Mr. Egan."

Egan had seen many things during his years as an attorney. This situation wasn't new. "Sydney grew up in this town, watched hundreds of young pilots come and go. She never intended to get involved with one. For her to break that conviction must have taken a special man. I wish the two of you had had more time before your transfer to Texas, but wishing won't change a darn thing now." He pushed some papers to Trey. "Read these. They have to do with transferring parental rights to you, as well as some other legal papers that I must file. I assume you'll want to change his last name to MacLaren?" Trey nodded, and Egan continued. "Take your time. I'm going for some coffee. Would you like anything?"

Trey was already halfway down the first page but looked up. "No, thank you." He took a deep breath and continued.

Trevor Trey MacLaren Powell was used throughout and was on the birth certificate. She had named him as the father. He guessed he'd change it to *Trevor Trey Powell MacLaren*. He felt it right to keep Sydney's name attached to their son.

Egan walked back in as Trey finished the last document.

"Is there any chance I can see Sydney?"

"I'm sorry, but Sydney specifically asked that you not visit her. She...well, she isn't in the best shape. She mentioned something about you remembering her the way she looked that night and not how she looks now."

Trey thought back on that night. Sydney was a stunning young woman, vivacious, smart, and funny. He glanced at Egan, his strained features signaling the sadness he felt. "I understand. Are there photos, anything you can give me that I may keep for Trevor?"

"Yes, she made provisions for all of that, including family medical history and information about his relatives on her side. But I have to tell you, they're a strange bunch. Live way up north and haven't seen Sydney in years. None of them have ever acknowledged Trevor. I don't expect they'll have much to offer."

Trey didn't understand that kind of family, yet he knew they existed.

Egan stood. "Are you ready to meet your son?"

"As ready as I can be, sir."

He opened his office door. "Connie?"

A young woman Trey remembered meeting that night, walked into the room carrying a fidgeting youngster with dark hair and striking blue eyes. Trey's hands turned clammy and sweat broke out on his forehead. *My son.*

"Hello, Trey. You probably don't remember me..."

"Yes, Connie, I do remember you." His eyes flicked to hers then moved back to focus on Trevor.

"I'm sure you aren't aware, but Sydney and I have been best friends since we were in kindergarten. We've been roommates for over five years, so I've been helping out with Trevor."

"You were with her during the pregnancy?"

"The whole time." She walked up to stand within a foot of Trey. "This is Trevor. He's almost fifteen months old, aren't you, Trevor?" Connie smiled at the boy, who looked at Trey, then buried

51

his head in Connie's neck. She turned a little so he could see Trey. "Trevor, this is your daddy." She knelt to place Trevor on the floor. "He's been walking for months, running actually. You'll see. He's a great kid and real active."

Trevor stared up at Trey, not smiling or frowning, just looking. Trey dropped to his knees so he was at eye level with his son.

"Hello, Trevor. It's good to meet you." He held out his hand for Trevor, but his son turned toward Connie and wrapped his arms around her legs.

"Now, Trevor, honey, this is your daddy. Say hi to him, sweetie." She pulled his small arms from her and turned him to face Trey.

"Dada," Trevor said but didn't move.

"That's right, son. I'm your daddy." Trey's chest tightened and he found it hard to take a breath.

"Sydney found a photo of you online with a group of other pilots, when you received your wings. I blew it up and have been pointing to you and telling Trevor you're his daddy. He started saying Dada just last week when I would hold up the picture."

"Dada," Trevor repeated, as if he were testing the word and trying to decide if he liked it.

"Yes, that's right." Trey held out his arms, hoping Trevor would come forward.

Trevor looked up at Connie.

"It's okay, honey. He's your daddy."

Trevor took a tentative step forward, raised his arms, and was swept into a hug by his father.

Trey held him, then stood. His son seemed solid, and heavy. He held Trevor away from him a few inches. "You are a big boy, aren't you, son?"

Trevor giggled, then laid his head on Trey's shoulder.

Oliver Egan cleared his throat. "Why don't you three take some time and get Trevor comfortable. Take a walk, get some food, then come back up here and we'll finish up."

The three walked outside. Connie pointed toward a small park a block away. Trey set Trevor down and he dashed toward an area meant for toddlers a few feet away. The adults sat on a bench, saying nothing, watching Trevor move from one large toy to the next.

"This must be hard for you," Trey finally said. He could see how much Trevor loved Connie, and it appeared she felt the same for him. "I can't thank you enough for all you've done."

Connie knew she'd tear up if she wasn't careful. The last thing she wanted was for Trevor to see her cry. She looked at Trey. "It's been wonderful. He's a great kid, and I love him like he was my own son."

"You're welcome to see him anytime. Just let me know." This was all new territory for Trey. He wanted to do right by Sydney and Connie, while he built a home for Trevor.

"How will you do it? Raise him, I mean, with your flying?"

"I'm fortunate in that I have two good friends who are roommates. It will be a guy house for sure, but he'll get lots of attention. We have two neighbor ladies, a couple of doors down, who asked if they could help out. They're sisters, both widows with grown children." He paused, wondering how much she knew about his family.

Connie watched him struggle with something, believing she knew what it might be. "You know, Sydney did a lot of research on you and your family. She wanted to be sure Trevor would be okay." She took a deep breath, thinking of her closest friend and that she'd be losing both Sydney and Trevor within a short time. "Anyway, she realized that financially, you're probably in good shape."

Trey pursed his lips. He never thought much about what he was worth. In his mind, it was just a number and didn't amount to anything, unless he'd earned it.

"My parents divorced a few years ago. My dad, Heath MacLaren, remarried just last weekend. Annie is a great woman. Trevor will have wonderful grandparents, aunts, uncles, cousins—it's almost overwhelming when I think about it." Trey tried to smile but couldn't quite manage it.

"And you? No wife, fiancée, girlfriend?"

Trey's stomach twisted at the thought of Jesse and how she'd walked out. He knew she had her reasons and if he gave it enough thought, he might find that they made sense. Right now, however, the pain of her leaving was still too new.

"No, none of the above, which is for the best. I need to focus on Trevor. I've got a two week leave arranged so the little man and I can get to know each other. I, uh, I hope he's okay with me."

Connie couldn't miss the anxiety in Trey's voice. "Are you kidding? Trevor will love you, and he'll adjust to you just fine. You'll see."

Chapter Seven

Connie had insisted that Trey spend the night at the place she rented with Sydney, so he could be around Trevor during dinner, bath, story, and bedtime. Trey watched, fascinated at how easy Connie made it all look.

"That boy likes just about anything you put in front of him. Not much he won't put in his mouth, except the smell or taste of bananas makes him run. Other than that, you're pretty safe." Connie finished clearing the table while Trey did the dishes. "I've packed his clothes and toys." She pointed to some boxes near the front door. "Do you need the furniture?"

"No, I think I'm good on the furniture. Plus, my folks are setting up a room for him at the ranch."

"Guess he'll have his own little pony real soon," Connie said, watching as Trevor played on the floor near them.

"Well, it works a little differently in our house. He'll have to prove he can take care of a pony before he gets his own."

Connie was surprised. From what she'd learned, the MacLarens could afford whatever they wanted. "So you don't have help? Cooks, maids, and such?"

Trey chuckled. "Oh, there's a cook and a housekeeper, but everyone has their own work, deadlines, and such. There are no free rides in my family." He paused. "Of course, Trevor will live with me, and I can assure you, we don't have a cook or a maid, unless you count the pathetic meals prepared by three bachelors."

It was Connie's turn to laugh. "Hey, I'd take a bachelor who could cook any day." She knelt and scooped up Trevor. "Bath time, big guy."

Trey watched, memorizing as much as he could about Trevor's routine. He hoped they'd be able to stick to it in California.

Trevor had fallen asleep within two pages of the story Connie had read. She'd offered to let Trey read to him, but he'd declined. This was Connie's last night with Trevor and he didn't want to take it from her.

By nine o'clock the next morning, Connie, Trevor, and Trey were at the airport. She met Robert and Todd, then watched everyone board. She stood on the tarmac as they took off, waving, and hoping Trevor could see her. Connie turned toward the visitor parking area and walked slowly to her car. She climbed inside, put the key in the ignition, covered her face, and cried.

******

Fire Mountain, Arizona

Heath, Annie, Jace, Caroline, and Cassie were standing and waving when the plane touched down. Trey descended the stairs with Trevor's small arms wound tightly around his neck.

"Easy, son. Don't strangle your daddy," Trey whispered.

Within a minute he was standing in the middle of a circle, all eyes on Trevor, his son's arms closing more tightly around him.

"Goodness, Trey. Trevor is the exact image of you when you were his age," Caroline's eyes focused on Trevor as she reached out to lightly stroke the boy's arm.

Heath just stared, a lump in his throat keeping him from speaking. Caroline was right—Trevor could have been Trey all those years ago. He watched as his son held his grandson, and damned if tears didn't blur his vision.

"Is it okay if your grandpa holds you, Trev?" Trey asked.

Trevor pulled his head away from Trey to look at the tall man standing next to him. Trevor studied Heath a moment before reaching his arms out. His grandfather took him in his arms, easing the tension that they all felt.

******

Trevor had eaten, taken his bath, and gone to bed with little fuss. He was proving to be a real trooper. Annie descended the stairs with Trey after watching the routine and offering a few encouraging words.

"How'd it go?" Heath asked. Everyone except Cassie had gone home, and they were now relaxing in the great room.

"Wonderful. Trey's a natural." Annie shared a look with Trey, then settled next to her husband on the large sofa.

Trey grabbed a beer before sitting in a nearby chair and stretching out his long legs. "I'm bushed. A day at the base isn't nearly as exhausting as running after Trevor. That kid can go." Trey took a long drag of his beer, then offered a tired grin.

"How is Jesse doing?" Annie asked. "I know you said she wasn't able to make the wedding, but I wondered how she's handling your new fatherhood."

"Not well, I'm afraid. She moved out."

"Moved out? Did she give a reason?" Annie looked to Heath, who gave her a warning look. "Of course, you can tell me to mind my own business. I won't take offense."

Trey leaned forward, resting his arms on his legs, and holding the bottle of beer between his hands. "She said it would be tough enough for Trevor and me to get settled without a woman being around. She felt it wasn't wise to have him get used to her being there, looking to her as another mother, because if things didn't work out between us, she thought it would be hard on Trevor." Trey took a deep breath and blew it out, then shifted back into the chair, raising his legs to rest on the ottoman. "I don't know. Maybe she's right."

"Maybe." Annie still thought Jesse's reaction was severe, but it was her decision to make. "Trevor is young. You know, children don't remember much before they're three and a half to four years old. It's sad, but the truth is, he won't have memories of Sydney. He'll know her only through any pictures and letters you might have. What I'm trying to say is, Jesse made a good point, yet I'm not sure it makes complete sense, given that Trevor's so young." She took a sip of her wine. "Do you plan to keep seeing each other?"

"No, and that's my doing. I got to the airport after your wedding and she'd sent Reb to meet me so that she could arrange her new living situation. She walked into the house with two other pilots and told me she was moving out. Honestly, I didn't hear much after that." He finished his beer. "I told her goodbye, then I left."

"Nothing since?"

"Not a word." He pushed up from his chair and stretched. "Well, I'm beat. See you two in the morning."

"Do you need help with Trevor tonight?" Heath asked.

"Nope, I have it covered. Goodnight."

******

Trey spent the next few days making sure everyone at the ranch met Trevor and that his family spent considerable time with him. Everybody knew there'd come a time when Trey would need to bring Trevor out for an extended stay.

His family was great, offering all kinds of support. Cassie, a freshman at Arizona State, had even offered to attend the local community college for two years, then transfer back to ASU, so that she'd be available to help. Heath had put an immediate stop to that line of thought.

Trey had spent a couple of nights out with his buddies, hooking-up with some old high school friends who still lived in the area. For the most part, he just hung out with them, talked, played pool, and caught up on everything he'd missed. By the end of the week, Trey felt a lot better about his new life as a father and pilot, feeling he could successfully juggle both.

Five days later, Trey carried Trevor up the stairs into the waiting plane. He settled in one of the comfortable leather seats and held Trevor on his lap. After a while, he set him on the floor to let him explore. Trey let his head fall back against the seat, while keeping an eye on his son. He thought about Jesse's reasons for leaving—at least, the reasons she'd given him. Trey couldn't shake the feeling that she'd decided to change course and was already seeing someone else, perhaps another pilot.

He watched Trevor play with a small ball that Heath had given him, and resolved to push thoughts of Jesse from his mind. He needed to concentrate on Trevor and his career, and free the memories he held of the woman he thought he'd marry.

******

Reb, Paul, Trey, and Trevor fell into a comfortable routine in their male only home. Trey had one more week of leave, which allowed him to get Trevor used to the widows down the street.

Alice Jones and her sister, Berta Banks, lived together and liked nothing more than to keep watch on the neighborhood and its children. Both had grown up in south central Los Angeles, but escaped, as they liked to say, when each married businessmen from out of the area. Alice settled in Sacramento and Berta in Bakersfield. Both had been widowed the same year and decided to buy a place together.

The sisters were firm believers in the concept that is takes a village to raise a child, although Trey thought of it as nothing more than friends looking out for friends, the same as it had always been. He'd take Trevor over each morning around ten, head to the gym, run errands, then pick up his son around one o'clock, in time for his nap. Reb and Paul would roll in about four in the afternoon and instantly vie for the position of most favored uncle status.

Trey would watch the two roll around on the floor with Trevor, twirl him in the air, and take him outside to meet the neighborhood dogs. It didn't take Trevor long to discover that his favorite

62

game was throwing a ball for the dogs to retrieve. He'd laugh and roll around on their grassy front yard, curling into himself to hide the ball from the various mutts that populated the area.

******

Jesse rested her back against the pillow and stretched out her legs. She'd been to the gym earlier, but felt the need for extra stretching, plus a few more abs—anything physical that would keep her mind off Trey.

"Hey, Jesse," Benny, one of her roommates, called. "Dinner in thirty."

"I'll be there," she called back, and continued her workout. She'd replayed their conversation over and over, wishing she'd waited until after Trey had brought his son home to make a decision to stay or leave. She'd panicked and overreacted, which was uncommon for her—except when emotions were involved. Jesse's heart ached when she thought of how it had ended. She'd picked up the phone several times, wanting to ask him to forgive her for the stupid way she'd acted. She wanted another chance. Each time she'd hung up before dialing, not wanting to hear his rejection.

"Jesse. Ten minutes."

"On my way." She jumped in the shower and was down the stairs in eight minutes, just in time to set the table, pull out drinks, and put on some music.

"About time you got out of the room and into the land of the living," Benny Ramirez joked, as he placed steaming tortillas into a warmer.

"What are you talking about? I'm always on for dinner. I'd even cook, if the two of you would trust me," Jesse threw back. It was a running joke that she didn't know how to make anything except for KFC, Subway, and Olive Garden take out. The last always made her other roommate, Anthony Bertani, cringe. Even though he occasionally ate at the well-known chain, his Italian heritage wouldn't accept anything other than pure, homemade food, like his Tuscan-born mother made, when he cooked for his roommates.

The three men settled into chairs and dished out the chicken tamales with rice and beans. Benny was a good cook, had saved money during high school while working in a small Mexican restaurant, and enjoyed just about everything he put into his mouth. How he stayed wiry-thin was a constant question.

"You know, Jesse," Tony ventured. "You should break down and call the guy. He's a good man." Tony shoveled a forkful of beans and rice into his mouth.

"He's right," Benny chimed in. "Trey's a straight shooter. You caught him unaware by just taking off." He held up his hand when Jesse started to protest. "Look, we don't want you to move out, just make things right with MacLaren. You know you want to." Benny wiggled his eyebrows at her as he took a slug of his favorite beer.

Jesse set down her fork and crossed her arms. "You're both right, okay. It's just not that simple."

"Of course it is," Tony threw out. "According to Reb and Growler, he's been back almost a week."

"I heard." She missed her ex-roommates more than she'd ever imagined. Tony and Benny were great, but they weren't family, not the way Reb, Paul, and Trey had been. Of course, Trey had been much more.

"Well?" Benny asked.

She glared at him. "Fine. I'll call him, but not until he's back on base. He's got enough to think about right now." Jess didn't add that she wasn't at all sure he'd be thrilled to get a call from her. It was her turn to suck it up and take a risk. Anyway, Jess rationalized, she couldn't hurt any worse than she already did.

Chapter Eight

As his last week of leave ended, Trey felt good about his situation and the home he was making for Trevor. Returning to the base on Monday morning wasn't the traumatic event he'd envisioned it would be.

"Thanks again for watching Trevor. I'll see you about four this afternoon." Trey waved to the sisters as he climbed into his truck.

He was halfway through his first day back when something felt wrong. He stopped what he was doing and tried to figure out what was amiss. Then it hit him—Trevor. He wasn't used to being away from him for more than three hours. This would be at least nine. He smiled to himself, shook off the feeling, and focused on what needed to be completed before heading home.

Trey stood next to his truck, talking with Reb and Paul, who'd parked beside him, when he saw a familiar figure walk across the lot. Jesse shifted her gaze, then stopped when she recognized him. Trey swung his eyes back to Reb, doing his best to ignore the instant pain that rocked him at the first sight of her in three weeks. He shifted so that his back was toward her.

Jesse got the message loud and clear. He had no interest in reconnecting. She knew him well enough to understand that Trey had an amazing ability to focus on his objective and not let anything stand in his way. That trait, coupled with his aptitude as a pilot and his leadership skills, had earned him his Lieutenant rank ahead of many others.

She continued toward her Jeep, ready to climb in, when she heard her name.

"Hey, Outlaw!" It was Reb. "How are you?"

She waved. "Good, Reb. I'm good."

"See you around?" Reb yelled back.

"Sure. Around." She sat down, closing the car door behind her. Jesse owned a well-used Jeep that was beginning to show signs of age. It needed a new battery, new tires, a paint job, and a lot more. For now, the battery and tires took precedence. She inserted the key into the ignition and turned it. Nothing. She tried once again and got the same distinctive sound, telling her the battery was dead. *Damn, not now.* She reached for her phone to call AAA, when someone tapped on her window.

"Need a jump?" Paul asked, as Reb stood beside him. Trey was nowhere in sight.

"That'd be great."

Ten minutes later, Paul was curling up his jumper cables. "You know, Jesse, you should call the guy."

"Who?"

"Don't feed me that crap. Trey. If it weren't for Trevor, he'd be a complete A-hole to live with."

She looked to Reb.

"Sorry, Jesse, but he's right. You have to com-mu-ni-cate with that guy, and soon." He enunciated each syllable and narrowed his eyes at her.

She glared at them before rifling a hand through her short hair. "Yeah, well, it's complicated."

"Pick up the damn phone and call him. It's not that hard," Paul growled.

Jesse shoved both hands into her pockets. "You two sound like Benny and Tony."

"Well, there you have it. Four guys on the same page." Reb clasped her shoulder.

"I'm out of here. You coming, Reb?" Paul asked as he turned toward his truck.

"Let me know if you need a pep talk before making the call." Reb turned to follow Paul, saluting her before they drove off.

Jesse climbed back into the seat and gripped the steering wheel with both hands. It would be easier to fly into enemy territory than to make that call. *How warped was that?* Jesse thought as she pulled out of the lot.

******

Two more days passed and Jesse still hadn't made a move. The guys just didn't understand how hard it was for her to reach out—not just to Trey, but to anyone. It was Saturday. Jess had been running errands and decided to order a sandwich and take it to a local park. She needed some downtime to figure out what to do next.

Jess settled on a bench, watching the children play and the parents scurry around trying to keep up. She laughed at some of the antics and realized she couldn't remember ever going to a park with her father.

She'd grown up the only child of a New Orleans cop. Her mom had taken off when she was three and no one had ever heard from the woman again.

Their house was on the outskirts of the city, on a bayou off a long dirt road. Her grandmama's house was next door, or what you'd consider next door when the closest neighbor was half a mile away. Between her grandmama and her dad, she'd had a pretty good life, except for the women who'd come and go.

Her father was a good-looking, hardworking, and hard-drinking backwoodsman. The only reason he was a cop was to put food on the table, not because he loved it. The odd thing was, he was a real good cop and had the awards to prove it. But at the end of the day, more often than not, he'd walk into their house with a new woman following behind him. She'd stay for a few weeks, maybe a few months, then leave. Usually because Jesse's dad would tell her to go. Her grandmama told her once that he'd never gotten over her mama leaving them. Oh, he wanted a woman, but he might never trust one again.

Jesse had studied hard in high school, tutored other students, been involved in sports, and earned an appointment to the Naval Academy. Although she'd made a couple of friends, for the most part, she kept to herself, not trusting anyone enough to get too close.

She'd done well at the Academy. Upon graduation, Jess had been given a chance at pilot training, where she'd excelled. There were a few other pilots she'd hung out with, including Reb and Trey, yet she'd never let anyone get too close. She understood the psychology behind it—her mother abandoning them had caused an innate fear of close friendships. Trey had been her first, and only, relationship. She didn't need anyone to explain it to her—she needed a way to overcome it.

Somehow, over the years and long hours of training, Trey had worn down her defenses, until they were living together, sharing a bed, and falling in love. In all that time, she'd never shared much of her past with Trey, even though he'd been up front about his family, his parent's divorce, and his desire to return to the ranch after his obligation to the Navy was over.

If only she'd explained something about her childhood, about how she'd tried a couple of times to form a friendship with her father's female friends, only to have him break it off and ask the woman to leave. Each time, she'd folded a little more within herself, and ultimately decided that building any relationship with those women was senseless.

When she'd learned of Trey's son, her first reaction was to move out, spare the child any hurt if she and Trey didn't stay together. In all honesty, she didn't want to form an attachment to Trevor, then have Trey change his mind and ask her to leave. Even though most wouldn't suspect it, she was a sucker for children—always had been. She now realized it was all about protecting herself and not about her feelings for Trey or her desire to build a lasting relationship with him.

Jesse stopped her mental rambling, deciding it was time to head home. She walked into the house to the sounds of cheering and yelling. The television showed the Los Angeles Angels playing the Houston Astros. Five to four in the bottom of the seventh. The first game of a double-header. Benny sported an Angel's cap, while Tony wore an Astros t-shirt. It figured that they'd be on opposite sides.

"Pizza's in the kitchen," Tony called between plays.

"Papa John's?" Jesse teased.

"Hell, no. Homemade. What kind of a man do you think I am?"

She smiled and grabbed a plate, loaded it with three pieces of pizza, found a soda in the refrigerator, and joined the boys in the living room. She hung out with them until the end of the first game, then headed upstairs to shower. Once dressed, she walked downstairs to find Reb and Paul in the kitchen, loading up on what was left of the pizza.

"Hey, Reb, Paul. I didn't know you were coming over." She hugged both before grabbing a bottle of water.

"Tony called at just the right time. Trevor was fussy, his dad didn't know what to do, and, since it was Trey's night to cook, pizza at your place

71

sounded like a good alternative. Give him a chance to mellow out with Trev." Reb headed toward the living room.

"Have you talked to him yet?" Paul asked without preamble.

"No."

He shook his head and followed Reb toward the sounds of the baseball game.

Jesse leaned back against the kitchen counter, took a swallow of water, and tried to clear her mind. He was home with his son. Maybe she'd just drive over, see if Trey would let her inside. *What's the worst that could happen?*

******

"Dada!" Trevor chanted, for at least the tenth time. He stood in his crib, hands gripping one side, and bounced up and down, calling for his dad. A few nights before, it had been Mama over and over, which had been harder for Trey to handle.

Trevor had eaten his dinner, had a bath and story, yet refused to settle down and sleep. Trey would give his son five more minutes before cracking the bedroom door to peek inside.

Within three minutes the sounds had ceased. Trey bounded up the stairs, hoping all he'd see was Trevor, asleep. Sure enough, his boy had worn himself out bouncing, finally dropping onto the mattress. He'd just pulled the blanket over Trevor's body when the doorbell chimed. Trey leaned down and kissed his son on the forehead, then crept out of the room.

He walked downstairs, feeling better than he had in several days. He'd done pretty good pushing Jesse from his mind, until then. At least he had reached the point where he'd accepted that it was over. He'd decided to look forward, not back, and made a vow to himself to never live with a woman again, unless they'd made a commitment to marry. No more trial runs. And no more female pilots. A stable, civilian woman was what he wanted for Trevor and himself.

"Coming," he called, as the doorbell sounded once more. He reached the door and pulled it open, stunned into silence by who stood outside.

"Hello, Trey." Jesse stood tall and looked him in the eyes.

He recovered quickly. "Jesse." He looked beyond her, but saw no one else. "What are you doing here?"

Her courage diminished as she realized he might not even allow her inside.

"Reb and Paul came over to watch the ballgame. It was loud, crazy, lots of testosterone, so I thought..." her voice trailed off.

"What? You'd come over here for old times' sake?"

She looked behind him. It hadn't occurred to her that he might have invited someone over. "I'm sorry. This probably wasn't a good idea—stopping by without calling." She turned to leave.

"Why did you come over? You generally have a plan for everything. This seems pretty spontaneous."

Jesse stopped, knowing he'd guessed right. She did have a plan but had lost her nerve as soon as he'd opened the door. Her heart had jumped into her throat at the sight of Trey. His deep gray t-shirt was drawn taut across his chest and tucked into tight fitting jeans. His dark hair was a little mussed, and the dark stubble on his face reminded her of the first time she'd met him, in the gym at the Academy. Her breath had caught then also, at the sight of the muscular, incredibly handsome, and somewhat dangerous looking midshipman.

Tonight it was by sheer will that she'd gotten out the first two words of a greeting.

She took a couple of steps toward him. "I guess I didn't think it through." She licked her lips, fortifying herself before looking into eyes that were set, hard. "The guys said you were here with Trevor. I'd been wanting to speak to you, to try to explain." She paused again, already sensing she'd made a huge mistake. "I guess I just wanted to see you."

Jesse could see the muscles of Trey's jaw tighten, knowing this was his way of dealing with difficult conversations. His narrowed eyes never wavered from hers. They'd turned a deep steel blue and she felt the coldness in them, even on this warm early summer night.

Trey wanted nothing more than to grab Jesse, haul her to him, and kiss some sense into her. His heart had stopped when he'd opened the door to

74

find her outside, after three weeks of nothing. He noticed her damp hair, could smell the scent of her shampoo, knowing she'd recently taken a shower. Memories of them naked, water sluicing over their bodies, assailed him, reminding Trey of what he'd lost. It also reminded him that their love was in the past. Over.

He softened his voice only a little. "Right now isn't the best time to talk. It's been a long day, Trevor just went down, and I'm dragging. Maybe another time."

Trey could see her struggle at hearing his dismissal. Truth was, he couldn't deal with listening to her excuses or rationalizations for walking out. She'd done it because that's what she'd needed to do, nothing more. Now he had to do what was best for him.

"All right, another time." She turned to go, then looked back over her shoulder. "Goodnight, Trey."

He stayed where he was, clutching the door handle so tight it felt like a death grip, watching as she got into her Jeep and drove away. As his breathing calmed and his heart settled, it dawned on Trey that perhaps he should have invited her in, listened to what she had to say. Maybe he owed her a chance to help him understand the reasons she'd left.

He'd struggled with their one-sided discussion the day he'd flown back from his father's wedding. Jess had calmly told him she was moving, as if it was not a big deal. He'd closed down, not allowing her to explain before grabbing his keys and leaving. In his mind, there was no justification for her walking out, making a unilateral decision that would tear them apart. After weeks of reflection, Trey *did* want to understand why, if for no other reason than to be able to move on.

Yet, when the opportunity had been upon him, he just hadn't been able to let her inside.

One thing had become immediately clear—he still loved her. Trey had expected his feelings to diminish after she'd switched living arrangements. He was disappointed in the reality.

Maybe, in time, they could talk it through, without the emotions that strummed through his body at the sight of her. For now, he needed to focus his life on Trevor and his career. All else would have to wait.

Chapter Nine

Two weeks had gone by since Jesse had stopped by Trey's house. She'd heard nothing from him, hadn't even seen him on the base. He'd dismissed her without a moment's hesitation. Jesse hadn't expected the immediate pain that ripped through her at his words. They weren't cruel or intended to hurt. They were uttered in the flat tone a homeowner would say to a door-to-door salesperson—*now's not a good time, maybe later*.

Jesse had driven home that night in a fog, taking her time, winding through different neighborhoods, her mind whirling from Trey's total lack of interest in seeing her again. She parked, noticing that Paul's truck was still outside. She opened the front door, surprised to learn that the baseball game had just finished. *Had she been gone that long?* Reb and Paul were standing, ready to take off. They'd exchanged goodnights, then headed home. Jesse was thankful she hadn't told them where she was going.

The time since had been busy, with little time to reflect back on that night. Flight exercises had ramped up over the past month, keeping everyone busy and allowing little downtime. With Paul in the same squadron, she was able to keep up on Reb—mention of Trey and Trevor was considered off limits.

"You going with us tonight?" Paul asked as they walked off the tarmac. Their squadron was meeting for dinner at a steakhouse a few miles from the base.

"Wouldn't miss it." Jesse was ready for a night away and a thick piece of red meat. Unlike many women, she ate whatever she wanted and until she was full. The job and daily gym routine kept her weight down and her head clear. "I'll clean up, then I'll see you there."

Two hours later, she stood at the bar with everyone else, listening to more hogwash than she'd heard in days. Regardless, they were a good group of pilots and Jesse considered herself fortunate to fly with them.

"Table's ready," someone called, and the group filed into the dining room.

"Over here, Jesse." Paul pointed to a chair between Nate Colvin and him.

She walked around the table and sat down, more than ready for food.

Everyone ordered and the banter continued as they ate their meals. She hadn't gotten to know Nate, so this gave them both a chance to get more acquainted.

"Where are you from?" Jesse asked as she slid a piece of steak into her mouth.

"Tulsa. Went to college at the University of Oklahoma and was in the ROTC program. That's what landed me here."

"Was it your plan?"

"Oh, yeah. Unlike you, I didn't get into the Academy, so I did the next best thing." He offered a half-smile and shrugged. "Where did you grow up?"

"A small town outside of New Orleans. I didn't know I wanted to be a pilot until my third year at the Academy."

"And was it the right choice?" Nate asked.

"Definitely. I feel like it's what I was born to do." Jesse finished her meal and pushed her plate away.

Nate signaled for another beer for each of them, then rested his arm on the back of Jesse's chair and leaned back in his own. "This is a nice place. Hadn't had a chance to come by before."

"I've been here a couple of times." Jesse thought of the nights Trey had brought her to the casual steakhouse—once with Reb and Paul as tag-a-longs. "You're right. It's a nice place."

"Hey, Reb!" Paul shouted across the noise of the dining room. "What brings you in here?"

Reb walked in with a stunning redhead on his arm. Jesse recognized her immediately as Shelly, Reb's regular date, and a new friend of Jesse's. "Daddy," his thumb pointed over his shoulder to the people behind him, "got a babysitter so we could venture out like adults." He laughed and performed a mock salute.

That's when Jesse noticed a petite, nice looking blonde walk in with her arm draped through Trey's. Jesse watched him glance around the room. When his eyes landed on her, he stopped. A moment passed before he moved on, as if she was nothing more than a distant acquaintance from his past.

"Well, I guess it's time I get going." Jesse set her half empty beer down and started to stand.

Paul's hand on her arm stopped her. "Don't. Wait a while so it doesn't look like you're leaving because of him." His voice was low, conspiratorial.

She nodded and sat back down.

The foursome was seated across the room, making it hard for Jesse to look up without staring directly at them. Unlike Reb's date, Shelly, who Jesse had met a couple of times, she'd never seen the woman who was with Trey. The four kept a running conversation, stopping only to order their meals. Trey looked rested, relaxed, and gorgeous. Jesse's heart twisted at the sight of him enjoying an evening out with another woman.

After an hour, she'd taken all she could. Jesse stood and started for the door.

"Wait up, Jesse. I'll go with you." Nate sauntered up behind her and they headed into the warm night air.

Trey took a long swallow from his water glass and watched Jesse walk out of the restaurant, followed by Nate Colvin. He knew the guy, liked him, and hoped he and Jesse were just friends and nothing more. The thought stopped him. He'd made the decision to forget about her, so why did it matter who she was with?

He hadn't wanted to go out with Reb and Shelly, preferring instead to spend time with Trevor, then kick back. The arrival of Shelly's cousin from San Diego changed his plans. Shelly wouldn't go out without Paige. Watching Reb grovel was ugly, so Trey had relented, forgetting that Paul and his squadron were going to the same steakhouse.

Paige was a nice lady, in her mid-twenties, and finishing graduate school in San Diego. She was quiet, not like Shelly who would go head-to-head with Reb on any issue, but the evening had been pleasant.

Thinking back, Trey knew he should've gone over and at least acknowledged Jesse. He felt like he was turning into a jerk where she was concerned. His family had taught him better. Trey had thought of calling her several times to meet at a local coffeehouse and clear the air. He hadn't been able to go through with it, figuring there was no sense in digging up emotions that were already buried.

******

"Fair warning, you two," Trey announced at dinner several nights later. "My stepbrother, Cameron, is driving over from San Francisco this weekend. He wants to see his new nephew."

"Sounds good. Doesn't he have a brother?" Reb didn't look up from his plate.

"Yeah, and a sister," Trey replied, while helping Trevor navigate a small spoon toward his mouth. "Eric is still recuperating from a motorcycle accident, and Brooke is in grad school in San Diego."

"Think she knows Paige, Shelly's cousin?" Reb asked.

"I asked Paige when we all went out. She hadn't heard of her. I think they're both at the same school, but it's a huge campus."

Trevor took that moment to show his dislike of the food Trey had provided, letting it run down his chin, shaking his head, and grimacing.

"Okay, Trevor. Let's try this again." Trey attempted to get his son to take another bite of the squashed banana before remembering what Connie had told him. No bananas. "Darn. Sorry, buddy. I'll get something else." He opened a cabinet door to grab another jar of food and start again.

Reb sat back in his seat, offering a wicked smirk. "Okay, so tell us about Brooke."

Trey cocked his head and stared at his roommate. "I don't think so."

"And why not?"

"First, she's a nice gal, but she's going through some stuff right now. She and I spoke when I went to my dad's wedding. And, no, I'm not going to share with you what she said. Second, she's my stepsister, and I'd be crazy to introduce her to you two miscreants."

Paul placed his hand over his heart. "Man, that's harsh."

"At least tell us if she's pretty," Reb persisted.

"Yes, in a girl-next-door kind of way." He grabbed his plate and walked to the sink, letting Trevor continue to play with his baby spoon and empty bowl. "And that's all I'm going to say."

"Okay, little man, it's my turn to give you a bath." Reb scooped up a giggling Trevor and headed upstairs. Most nights, Trey did the honors, but lately, Paul and Reb had begun pitching in, even reading to Trevor before Trey came up to say goodnight.

Trey dried his hands, grabbed a bottle of water, then settled into a large, comfortable chair in the living room. Paul followed him in and took a seat before punching the channel changer.

"Fishing channel?" he asked Trey.

Trey closed his eyes and nodded, not caring as long as he got to relax for ten minutes. They could hear the sounds of Trevor enjoying his bath—splashing and laughing. All three had learned to strip off their shirts when giving the kid a bath.

It had been several weeks since Trey had flown to Florida to pick up his son. He'd called Oliver Egan a couple of times, asking how Sydney was doing, hoping that there might be some improvement, yet knowing her situation was beyond human help. Mr. Egan had assured him that the doctors were keeping her as comfortable as possible. They didn't expect she'd last much longer.

Trey opened his eyes to glance at Paul, debating whether to say anything or keep his mouth shut. He was tired of keeping his thoughts bottled up.

"How's she doing?"

"Good." Paul didn't have to ask who Trey was referring to.

"Keeping up?"

"Better than that."

They fell silent for a long minute.

"And Nate Colvin?"

Paul did look up this time, confused by the question. "Nate? Yeah, he's good."

"He get along well with her?"

Now Paul got it. Trey must have noticed Nate and Jess at the base, joking and laughing. He knew there wasn't anything going on between the two, they were just friends. Paul wished Jesse and Trey would screw their heads back on and work this thing out. Paul was ready to get their old life back, plus baby. First, he wanted to mess with his hardheaded roommate.

"Other than he's got a hard-on for her, yeah, they get along great." Paul got the reaction he expected.

Trey's head snapped toward him. "That a fact?" Trey ground out.

"Pretty much. I don't think Jesse has a clue that she's causing the man great discomfort. She does her job and heads home." Paul clicked the channel changer a couple of times, settling on the Discovery channel. "Course, I did hear Tony and Benny talking about wanting a fourth roommate. I think Ben mentioned it to Nate."

"Shit," Trey muttered and pushed himself up from his chair. "I'm heading upstairs."

"Sure, man. See you in the morning." Paul hid a grin at the disgust in Trey's voice. He thought someone had to light a fire under one of them. Might as well start it now.

Chapter Ten

"Welcome, Cam." Trey opened the door, grabbed his stepbrother's hand, and pulled him into a brief hug. "Great to see you."

"Same here." Cameron looked around as he stepped into the small entry. "Nice place." He set his bag down.

"Thanks. What can I get you?" Trey asked.

"I'm good for now." He followed Trey toward the sound of a little boy's giggles. "Wow. So this is Trevor." Cam's eyes had grown wide as he took in the newest MacLaren. "Jesus, Trey, the kid looks just like you."

"Yeah, ain't it great?" Trey joked, and got a punch in his arm for the effort. "Go ahead, pick him up. He hasn't bitten anyone in several days."

Cam rolled his head in a circle to stretch the tight muscles, squared his shoulders, then leaned down. "Hey there, Trevor. I'm your Uncle Cameron. Can I hold you?"

Trevor's eyes darted to Trey, then back to Cameron.

"It's okay, Trev. Go ahead and let Uncle Cam pick you up."

Cam reached out his arms as Trevor reached for him. "Wow, you're a heavy little guy," he joked.

"Come on," Trey said, grabbing Cam's bag, "I'll show you where you'll be sleeping."

Paul and Reb had moved Trevor's crib into Trey's bedroom while Trey had made up the hide-a-bed in his son's room.

"You're in here. Hope that's okay." Trey dropped Cam's bag on the floor.

"Dada," Trevor squealed, reaching for his father.

"No, Trevor, it's not your bedtime. Uncle Cam is sleeping in here tonight. That all right?"

"Dada," Trevor repeated.

"Now you've heard about one-third of his vocabulary. He also says ball and down—sort of. The second one's not as clear. He also says Mama, but I haven't heard that one in quite a while."

"You mentioned when I called that she has terminal cancer. Must be hard," Cam said as they made their way downstairs and into the living room. He set Trevor on the floor and rolled a ball toward him.

"Ball," Trevor said and leaned toward the toy.

"Sydney, his mother, wouldn't let me see her when I went to pick up Trevor." Trey shoved his hands in his pockets and continued to stand, watching his son play with the ball. "Anyway, I've called a couple of times. She's still hanging on, but her attorney says they don't expect her to last much longer."

"Well, seems like this was a good time for me to drive over."

Both men looked toward the door at the sound of voices. Paul walked in, followed by Reb, Tony, Benny, and Nate.

Trey looked at Nate, his face impassive. He introduced everyone to Cam, scooped Trevor up from the floor, and strolled into the kitchen. "Who's here for dinner and who's not?" he called over his shoulder.

"We're heading out, Trey. Just stopped by to grab some things," Reb yelled back as he ran up the stairs.

"Yeah, big night out. Bowling." Paul grabbed a beer out of the refrigerator, popped the top, and took a long swallow. "Dinner at Bud's."

"Hey," Benny said, following Paul to the refrigerator. "I like Bud's."

"What more could a bunch of single guys ask for on a Friday night besides burgers and bowling? As long as there's beer with it, I'm fine." Nate leaned against a wall, crossing his arms over his chest, eyeing Trey. He knew the history Trey had with Jesse. Even though Nate liked Jesse and would love a chance with her, he knew it was out of the question. First, because they were in the same squadron, and second, because you just didn't do that to another pilot—not unless you were a complete jackass.

"All set," Reb called. "Good to meet you, Cameron."

"Same here," Cam called back as the five filed outside.

A couple of hours later, the two sat on lounge chairs on the back patio.

"Tell me what's happening with you and Jesse," Cam said after a while. Trey shot him a look. "Mom asked," Cam clarified and offered a half-smile.

"Ah, yes, that would make sense. Annie and Jesse struck up a friendship when we were out there a few weeks before the wedding." Trey rolled a bottle of water between his hands, then set it on a table next to his chair. "Things between us went to hell the day before we were supposed to fly out for the wedding."

"That's about the time you heard about Trevor?"

Trey nodded. "When I got back from the wedding, she moved out. Two of the guys you met tonight, Tony and Benny, are her new roommates. Rumor is that the third one, Nate, may be moving in also."

"No explanation?"

"None that I understood or wanted to hear. Something about not wanting Trevor to get attached to another woman, thinking she may be a mother replacement, and how he'd handle it if things didn't work out between us." He scrubbed a hand over his face. "Hell, I don't know, maybe she was right."

"Maybe," Cam replied. "But sounds to me like she wasn't as committed to the relationship as you were. Or she was just plain scared. You know, things moving too fast and all that."

"Maybe. She stopped by a few weeks ago, wanted to talk and try to explain. I blew her off."

Cam remained silent. His track record with women was spotty at best. His last one had ended about the same time as Trey's.

"I'm not great at this relationship stuff, but it seems to me you've got Trevor to think about, and a demanding job. It may not be your time."

Yeah, time, Trey thought. Cam may be right, yet Trey couldn't shake the feeling that he and Jesse weren't through. His gut told him what he really needed was to find a way to talk things through and see if they still had a chance at a future.

******

Trey, with Trevor in tow, gave Cam a tour of the base the following day, including a look inside his fighter jet.

"Cowboy. That you?" Cam asked when he saw the name on the outside of Trey's plane.

"Yeah. My call sign. Reb's is, for lack of imagination, Reb, and Paul's is Growler."

"Growler?"

"You'll get it if you spend any time around him." Trey grinned and walked toward another area to show Cam the helicopters. He knew Cam had his private pilot's license and had talked about getting one for helos, although Trey didn't understand why. As the head of the Information Technology department at a large company in the bay area, he couldn't see where Cam would have a use for it.

"These are something," Cam breathed out as he walked around the Sikorsky Seahawk, part of the Search and Rescue—SAR—team at the base. "Any chance I can see inside?"

Trey looked behind him and saw a civilian mechanic working on another helo. He signaled to the man.

"What can I do for you, Lieutenant?"

"Any problem showing my brother the inside of this one?"

"Don't see why not."

A couple of minutes later, Cam sat inside the large helo, fascinated by the controls, which were so much different from the small, fixed-wing planes he'd flown. After ten minutes, he climbed down, looking at the cockpit once more before turning to Trey.

"Thanks, man. That was great."

Trey could see the pleasure in Cam's face and wondered, once again, what had him so interested in helicopters.

"It's getting late. Best we get this big guy home and feed him, right, Trev?" Trey bounced his son a couple times in the air, initiating a surge of laughter that had the brothers grinning.

******

"Grab a seat and relax," Reb called from the kitchen as Cam, Trey, and Trevor walked in. "I've got dinner under control."

"Missed you at the ball game, Trey." Paul sat by the television, flipping from one channel to another.

"How'd you do?"

"Killed 'em. What else?" Paul never looked up. "It was a bitch though, without our best pitcher."

"Sounds like you survived and conquered," Trey commented as he took a seat and set Trevor on the floor.

"Played against Jesse's team."

That brought Trey's eyes up, but he didn't respond. She'd been a member of their softball team until she'd moved out. No one had asked her to change. As with all of her latest actions, she'd made the decision without a thought to anyone else.

"Glad you prevailed," Trey whispered as he watched Cam pull a ball from behind a chair and roll it to Trevor.

After lunch the following day, Trey watched Cam throw his bag into the back of his SUV.

"Thanks for having me," Cam said as he walked back to stand by Trey.

"Anytime. Maybe we can make this happen every few months. You come here or I'll drive over," Trey suggested.

"I'd like that." Cam clasped Trey's shoulder. "Take care of this little one." He smiled at his nephew before climbing behind the wheel. "Keep me posted," he called, knowing his meaning wasn't lost on Trey.

Chapter Eleven

Jesse let Shelly pull her through the women's department at a downtown store, trying to find the right dress for a dance the following weekend. It was an annual event, held at a local country club. Locals and base personnel were encouraged to attend the black tie event, and since it wasn't sponsored by the Navy, formal uniforms weren't required.

"Here we go," Shelly said when they'd gotten to the evening dress section. "What size?"

"A six, I guess. It depends."

Shelly whizzed through the dresses, looking at colors first, then style.

Jesse hadn't been dress shopping since she'd arrived at the base. She appreciated Shelly's efforts, but this just wasn't her thing.

"Try these, then this group." Shelly held up what she'd found.

"All those?" Jesse groaned.

"Every single one. Sometimes there's a sleeper that looks better on. You never know."

"Why can't I just wear my uniform? The invitations said formal military attire would be fine."

"Yes, and formal, non-military apparel is fine, too. This is your chance to flaunt your stuff."

Shelly knew Jesse didn't see herself as others did. She believed herself to be average in every way, except when she flew. Jesse had no idea how men's eyes followed her when she came into a room or passed by them in the store. At five-feet-six inches, she was slim, with a great shape. Her short, golden brown hair, and brown eyes with copper colored flecks, set off her smooth, creamy skin. The few freckles across her nose added character, although Shelly knew Jesse would just as soon get rid of them.

Jesse shook her head, grabbed the clothes, and found a dressing room.

She first slid into a slinky, black dress that fell to just below her knees. It had long sleeves and a scooped neckline. Jesse liked it, but Shelly had given it an immediate thumbs down. It was the only black dress in the bunch. Next was a teal green, followed by a deep peach, which Jesse liked—Shelly crinkled her face.

There were only three left. Jesse selected one of the red dresses. It was a strapless, floor length, chiffon sweetheart dress with a slit to her mid-thigh. It draped in front and back, and was, quite simply, the most gorgeous dress Jesse had ever seen. She took one more look, then walked out to show Shelly.

"Oh my." Shelly jumped up and put a hand to her mouth. "That is stunning." She cocked her head and moved around Jesse in a slow circle. "It doesn't need a thing done to it. It's perfect."

Thirty minutes later, they left the center with her red dress, new shoes, glittery shawl, and small handbag.

"Now, all you need is a necklace and earrings, and I have just the set." Shelly smiled at Jesse as they pulled out of the lot and drove to a small restaurant, popular with the locals.

"Turkey on wheat," Shelly ordered.

"The same for me," Jesse told the waitress and sipped at her diet soda. She liked Shelly and was grateful that Reb's friend had thought to invite her along to shop for dresses. Jesse would've opted for her dress whites, even though she knew most of the guys would be wearing civilian clothes as a change to the Navy formal wear they'd worn so much over the last several years.

Shelly kept up the small talk until their food arrived. They lapsed into silence before she broached the subject both knew had been hanging between them.

"I didn't get a chance to introduce you to my cousin, Paige, when we saw you at the steakhouse. I'm sorry if it was awkward for you."

"Don't worry about it. We all knew Trey would meet someone else. I just hadn't expected it to be quite so soon." Jesse had lost her appetite and played with the fries piled on her plate.

"They aren't a couple. Paige doesn't even live here." Shelly continued when she saw the confusion on Jesse's face. "Like I said, she's my cousin. She flew up from San Diego for a weekend, to get away from her grueling schedule. Paige is working on her doctorate. Poor thing never gets out, knows almost no one, and walks the beach alone for fun. What kind of a life is that?" Shelly ate the last bite of her sandwich and wiped her hands on a napkin.

"Not much, I guess." Other than flying, Jesse didn't have much of a life either.

"I told Reb that I would only go out if he found a date for Paige. He drafted Trey, who wasn't happy but played the gentleman anyway. She had a great time, Jesse, but there wasn't anything more to it."

Jesse looked out the window at the vast expanse of flat land. She could hear the occasional rumble of a semi, moving along the freeway. Other than that, it was a pretty quiet community.

"I'm here if you want to talk. I know it must be tough being around guys all the time, but you do have at least one female friend." Shelly offered a warm smile.

Jesse glanced at the woman across from her. Yes, Shelly was probably the one female friend she had, other than Anita, who was stationed at Virginia Beach. "It's my fault, not Trey's. I'm the one who walked out."

Shelly didn't respond, waiting for Jesse to continue.

"I went back to the house a few weeks later when I knew he was alone, and tried to explain. He brushed me off—wouldn't even let me inside."

Shelly rested her elbows on the table and leaned forward. "Reb says he's still in knots over what happened. That doesn't sound like someone who's over you."

Jesse thought about that for a long minute. "You should have seen his face the day I left. I'll never get that look out of my mind." She looked up. "I'd give anything to take that day back, to be the way we were."

The two sat in silence for several minutes, Jesse more playing with her fries than eating them, and Shelly sipping her drink.

Jesse pushed her plate away and let out a long breath. "I need to face reality. Trey isn't the kind to forgive and forget—at least not with me. Even if he gave me the chance to explain, it probably wouldn't make a difference. I need to accept the fact that he's moved on, and that's what I need to do too." Jesse grabbed her purse and stood.

"Well then, that's exactly what will happen Saturday night," Shelly replied, as they made their way outside.

******

"Who's watching the squirt tonight?" Reb fiddled with his tux. "Damn, I hate these things," he mumbled as he hooked the bow tie in place.

"But you look so handsome," Paul smirked, while he pulled on his coat.

"Stuff it," Reb replied.

"Did you ask me something?" Trey walked from the kitchen, holding Trevor.

"Who's watching Trev?"

"The twins, Marissa and Miranda, from down the street. The ones who watched him when we went to dinner at the steakhouse."

"Yeah, I remember," Reb replied. "You need me to go pick them up or anything?"

"Marissa said they'd walk over. It's only five houses away. They may take Trevor over there for a while. They'll let me know." Except for his jacket, Trey was already dressed. "You meeting Shelly there?"

"She's going, but nothing formal. It's not like we can't see other people."

"That so? And are you?" Paul asked.

"You know damn well I'm not. Hell, when would I find the time to meet someone else?" Reb complained.

"Or someone who's as much fun as Shelly? She must be a handful." Paul grinned and dashed upstairs.

Trey heard the doorbell and opened the door to see the twins standing outside, holding a large fabric bag full of toys. "Wow, you've come prepared." Trey let the two girls pass and followed them into the living room.

Trevor reached out to Marissa, who set him down beside the bag. He started to pull out brightly colored blocks and balls, giggling as his small hands found more treasure.

"That's it, Trevor. Have at it," Miranda said and sat down against the front of the sofa.

"He's had dinner, but still needs his bath." Trey slipped into his jacket and adjusted his tie.

"No problem, Mr. MacLaren. Baths are our specialty." Marissa glanced at her sister, Miranda, who nodded.

"You have my cell?"

"Yes, and Mr. Cantrell's and Mr. Henshaw's."

"Well, that's good." Trey hadn't known that Reb and Paul had provided their numbers also.

"You ready?" Reb called.

Trey picked up Trevor, gave him a kiss and hug, then handed him back to Miranda. "You be good," he said before leaving.

******

"Turn around one more time," Shelly instructed, watching as Jesse rotated again. "You look amazing."

"I look different, that's for sure." Jesse wasn't used to wearing makeup, high heels, or fancy jewelry. She fingered the necklace Shelly had let her borrow. The matching earrings were at least three inches long and glittered in the lamplight of Shelly's bedroom. Jesse's short, golden brown hair complemented the beautiful red dress, which fell off her shoulders.

"Different, are you kidding? You'll knock 'em dead tonight," Shelly laughed. "You ready?"

Jesse wrapped the shawl around her shoulders, picked up her small bag, and nodded.

The reception would start at six o'clock, followed by dinner, and dancing. Jesse followed Shelly up the steps of the country club and into the large room set aside for the event. Music was already playing, and the room was full of beautifully dressed women and men in tuxedos. Jesse could feel the butterflies in her stomach ease as she scanned the room and saw no sign of Trey.

"Let's find a table, then order drinks," Shelly suggested. She walked toward a table near the stage. "This looks like a good spot."

Jesse and Shelly set down their handbags before getting into the drink line.

Shelly introduced Jesse to several people she knew from her job as an assistant administrator at the community hospital. When the dinner chime sounded, they returned to their table to find that all the seats had been taken by two other couples and two single men, who were partners in a local construction company. One had a seat next to Shelly, while the other was next to Jesse.

"And what do you do, Jesse?" Alex Parker was an attractive man with dark blond hair, deep green eyes, and a dark tan. He and Miguel "Mike" Flores owned a large commercial building firm, specializing in government projects.

"I'm a pilot at the base." Jesse was used to stunned responses at her chosen career.

"That right?" Alex took a closer look at her. "I believe I've seen you on base. My company does a lot of the construction there. It's hard to miss a female pilot." His smile was warm, genuine. She liked Alex right away. "You graduate from the Academy?"

"Yes. Where are you from?" Jesse sipped her wine, then took another bite of sliced tri-tip.

"All over. My dad was in the Air Force, so we moved around a lot. So was Mike's. Our fathers were at the same base back east when we were in high school, so we ended up running into each other quite a bit. We both attended the University of Texas and finally made our way out here."

"Sounds like a great friendship."

"It is. We work well together, split up the operations so that we don't duplicate efforts. We've had the firm for a few years now." Alex set his wine glass down. "Would you like to dance?"

Jesse hadn't been prepared for the invitation, yet found herself accepting it. "Yes, I would." She took Alex's hand as he led her to the dance floor.

The band played a mix of old and new songs. She hadn't noticed how tall Alex was until he stood, but Jesse estimated him to be at least six-feet-three or four inches, muscled, with broad shoulders.

"So, tell me why someone who looks like you is here alone," Alex said as he led them around the floor.

Jesse laughed. "Well, you have to understand that this," she looked down at her dress, "isn't the normal me. I work with men, have two male roommates, and dress in flight suits most of the time. I'm not what most men would consider their ideal woman."

Alex looked down at her. "I hope you're kidding, because I can't imagine anyone like you going unnoticed."

Jesse smiled up at him. "Thank you." She thought a minute, then decided to forge on.

"Actually, the relationship I was in ended a few weeks ago. My friend, Shelly, convinced me to start testing the waters."

"Well, you're doing a real fine job, Jesse."

"And you? How come you're here with your business partner?"

Alex was quiet for a moment before answering. "My wife and I are separated. She's a Texas girl and didn't quite take to California. I'm still hopeful we can work it out."

The sadness in his eyes tore at Jesse. She understood that sadness. "I'm sorry. How long has she been gone?"

"About six months. My company is in partnership with our original boss in Texas—my wife's father." He let out a long breath. "It's complicated."

"Children?"

"Thank God, no."

"I truly hope you can work things out."

"Yeah, so do I."

They danced one more song. Alex was good at both dancing and conversation, and Jesse found herself enjoying the evening more than she expected. At one point, she looked across the dance floor to see Shelly dancing with Alex's partner, Mike, and laughing.

******

Trey, Reb, and Paul had entered the room just as everyone was being seated for dinner and took a table at the back. Trey scanned the room until his gaze landed on Jesse, at a table near the front. He'd watched her talk and laugh with the man next to her, and Trey found himself wondering if he was her date.

"You see that?" Reb nudged him and nodded toward the dance floor.

"You mean Shelly?" Trey asked.

"Shelly and Jesse. Looks like I may have to fight my way to get a dance with Shel. But, Jesse, who would have thought she could clean up like that?"

Trey's gaze fixed on Jesse. He'd thought the same thing when he'd seen her stand and walk onto the dance floor. His mouth had gone dry and his hands had balled into fists at his sides. She was stunning, to the point he found it hard to breathe. He needed some air.

"Where you headed?" Reb asked, his eyes never leaving Shelly and her partner.

"Outside. I'll be right back." Trey made his way around the tables to an exit leading to a large patio with a view of the manicured golf course. He stood near the railing, his hands resting on the top rung, while he scanned the view. Trey heard the door open and close, hoping that whoever it was would leave him alone. He needed space.

"Hey."

He knew that voice. His stomach tightened, and he turned to see Jesse walk toward him.

"Hello, Jesse."

"I saw you come out here. Let me know if you'd rather be alone, I'll understand." Jesse's heart jolted as she fought an overwhelming need step closer to him.

Alex had been escorting her back to their table, when she saw Trey walk around the room and slip outside. She'd taken a deep breath, excused herself, and followed him.

Trey didn't respond, finding it hard to take his eyes off her. He tore his gaze away and focused on the long fairway with trees edging both sides, trying to calm his racing heart. "You look beautiful tonight." His voice was low, thick.

Jesse had stepped up beside him. "Thank you." She placed her hands on the rail next to his.

Neither said a word for long minutes. Other than the music from inside, it was a quiet night. They could occasionally hear the sound of a dog barking in the distance or a car pulling out of the parking lot.

"Who's your date?" Trey finally asked.

"My date?"

Trey glanced at her. "The man with blond hair sitting next to you?" His words were clipped, coming out harder than intended.

"Alex? He's not my date. I came with Shelly. Alex and his business partner, Mike, came together. I guess their firm is doing the construction we see around the base." Jesse wanted to put her hand on his arm, but fear of him shaking it off stopped her. "He and his wife are separated. It's pretty obvious he still cares a great deal about her."

Even though they stood on an expansive outside patio, Trey felt the space closing in on him.

He glanced at her, noting again how stunning she looked, her beautiful skin, and her full, red lips. He needed to either pull Jesse to him, wrap his arms around her, and capture her mouth with his, or leave. The decision was made for him.

The door opened. "Trey? You left your phone on the table..." Paul started before he saw Jesse. "I'm sorry to interrupt, but it's Mr. Egan." He handed the phone to Trey.

Trey took it and walked a few paces away, turning so his back was to Jesse and Paul.

"Yes, I understand. I'd like to fly back, if you think that would be all right?" Trey paused. "Wednesday. Yes, I have it." More silence. "Thanks, Mr. Egan." Trey closed the phone and slid it into his pocket. He didn't turn back toward them right away.

"You okay, man?" Paul asked.

"Yeah, I'm fine. That was Sydney's attorney." He glanced at Jesse. "She is, or was, Trevor's mother. She passed away a couple of hours ago. He thought I should know." He took a slow breath. "I need to make arrangements to fly back for the services."

"Sorry, Trey. I'll get Reb and we'll take off." Paul walked back into the room, closing the door behind him.

Jesse stood rooted in place, seeing the sorrow on Trey's face, wanting to help, yet not knowing what to say.

"Is there anything I can do?" she finally asked.

He looked up. "No, nothing. I better get going."

Trey turned toward the door, leaving Jesse to stand there alone, feeling hollow and lost.

If she'd only stayed with him, he'd have turned to her for comfort, wanted her to be with him. Now, he needed nothing—at least, no comfort she could provide.

She waited a few minutes, then returned to the party to look for Shelly. She saw her on the dance floor. When the music stopped, Shelly hurried over, an expectant look on her face.

"Did you find Trey, talk with him?" She'd hoped Jesse and Trey may have been able to start mending things, but the look on Jesse's face said otherwise.

"No. He got a call from the attorney for Trevor's mother. She passed away a few hours ago. He needs to fly out for the services." She took a steadying breath, squared her shoulders, and tried for a smile, which failed miserably. "I offered to help, but of course, he refused. The look on his face, so determined and strong, told me what I needed to know. He doesn't need me, Shel. I'm not going to hope for a change of heart any longer." Her voice hardened as she spoke. "I'm a damned good pilot, and have a great career doing something I love. I'm not going to let this get to me any longer." She stared past her friend, focusing on a blank wall—anything, to regain her composure and not think of Trey.

Shelly didn't believe a word of it. "All right, I'm ready to take off. You with me?"

Jesse nodded, then walked to their table, thanked Alex for the dances, and grabbed her purse.

"Jesse?" Alex stood next to her. "I'm not looking for anything, but if you ever want to talk, grab lunch or dinner, let me know." He handed her his card.

She took it and smiled. "Thanks, Alex. I'd like that." At least the night had offered one positive outcome.

Chapter Twelve

"We've got the sisters lined up each morning, the twins after school, and Paul and I at night. Don't worry. You're only gone a few days. Piece of cake." Reb held Trevor while Trey finished packing for the flight to Pensacola.

Trey looked at his son, knowing he'd be safe with his friends, yet feeling something was amiss. He'd gone through a mental checklist and everything had been handled. Still, he felt a sense of unease.

He wasn't looking forward to the trip, yet his conscience made it mandatory. Besides, it would give him a chance to see Connie, provide some pictures of Trevor he hadn't sent via email, and perhaps learn more about Sydney.

"Guess I'd better get going." He leaned down and placed a kiss on Trevor's forehead, stroked a finger down the toddler's cheek, and wondered, for the millionth time, how he'd become so attached to his son in so short a time.

"Come on, Cowboy," Paul yelled from the seat of his truck.

"See you Thursday." Trey walked outside to his waiting ride.

Reb picked up Trevor's hand and moved it up and down. "Say, bye-bye Dada," he prompted Trevor.

"Dada," Trevor giggled out.

Trey heard and turned back, waving at his young son, before disappearing into the cab of the truck.

He hadn't contacted his dad about using the company jet, believing this was something he had to handle alone. He loved his family. Even though he relished his job as a pilot, he missed the land, the daily demands of running a ranch, and the familiarity of those he'd known his entire life. Kicking back at the end of the day with fellow pilots was different than doing the same on his dad's patio, a fire blazing in the large fire pit, his sister running in to give him a kiss and tell him about her latest adventures.

Trey spent the trip doing mental gymnastics, between images of Sydney, Trevor, and Jesse. He'd felt an instant rapport with Sydney and had thought, much like Mr. Egan had stated, it was too bad he and Sydney hadn't been able to spend more time together. She'd given him a wonderful son, who he adored. So many of the circumstances seemed wrong, yet he knew life didn't fall into easy boxes that mere humans could figure out.

An image of Jesse surrounded him. Trey remembered the impact she'd had on him when he'd seen her walk onto the dance floor. His breath had caught at how achingly beautiful she looked. He'd always thought of her as pretty, but that night, she'd been stunning to the point of causing his chest to squeeze in pain.

He tried to stretch out his long legs in the tight aisle seat in the coach section. The plane was full, offering little chance for true solitude. He leaned his head back, closed his eyes, and tried to recall the last few times he'd seen Jesse.

The day he'd flown back from the wedding and she'd told him of her decision to move out. He'd been too stunned to discuss her reasons, only comprehending that she was bailing but not much else. She'd then tried to stop by when it was only he and Trevor in the house. Again, he'd shut her out, not wanting to hear excuses or rationalizations.

The last time was at the dance. Trey knew she'd come outside to see him, perhaps to talk. He'd been standing on the patio, chastising himself for pushing her away and not allowing her a chance to explain, then she'd appeared beside him. He couldn't take his eyes off her and was about to give in to his need to pull her to him, bury his hands in her soft hair, and kiss her until neither of them could breathe, when Paul had appeared.

The news of Sydney's death shouldn't have stunned him, yet it did. He'd hoped for a different outcome, knowing it was beyond his power. When he'd hung up from the call and turned around, he'd seen Jesse standing next to Paul, waiting for him. She'd offered to help, and again, he'd pushed her attempt to extend an olive branch aside. He'd seen her eyes close and her features still, as if she'd finally accepted there was nothing she could do to reach him. His heart constricted at the memory of the look on her face, and Trey knew that if they were ever going to make things work, it was now up to him.

It was evening when the plane touched down in Pensacola. Trey picked up a rental car and drove straight to his hotel, stopping long enough to call Reb and let him know he'd made it.

His room was comfortable, sparse, and only fifteen minutes from the church where Sydney's services would be held. Trey grabbed a quick dinner, then kicked back, fidgeting. He wasn't used to having nothing immediate to do. He checked his watch—eight o'clock, not so late. He grabbed his phone and dialed Connie's number.

"Hello?"

"Connie?"

"Yes, this is Connie." Her voice sounded tired, strained, and Trey wondered if he'd made a mistake.

"It's Trey MacLaren. I just got in and thought I'd let you know."

"Trey, it's good to hear from you." She sounded genuinely pleased he'd called. "Where are you staying?"

He gave her the name of the small hotel. "I know it's a little late, but if you're not too tired, how about meeting me for a drink?"

She took a moment to answer, and Trey wondered again if he shouldn't have bothered her. "Give me forty-five minutes, and let me know where."

He chuckled. "I was hoping you could suggest a place."

They settled on nine o'clock at a restaurant and bar a few blocks from his hotel. Trey looked forward to seeing her.

******

"Trey."

He heard his name and saw Connie waving from a table near the window. She stood to give him a brief hug.

"I'm so glad you decided to come. Mr. Egan let me know to expect you at the services. I know it must've been hard not being able to speak to Sydney directly before she—" Connie's words trailed off as her throat closed with emotion.

Trey placed a hand on hers and squeezed. "I wanted to be here." He let his hand drop away. "Besides, I thought you'd like to have some actual pictures of Trevor that you could hold in your hand." He handed her the large envelope he'd brought.

She didn't wait. Connie opened the envelope and was looking at the photos in seconds. Trey noticed the emotions passing over her face as she held each one. She laughed at a couple, smiled at others, and showed no emotion for a few.

"Are these your roommates?" She held up one with two unfamiliar men.

"That's them. Reb's on the right and Paul's on the left. Poor kid's going to grow up thinking he has three fathers."

"You mentioned another roommate when you were here—a female pilot, but I don't see her in any of the pictures."

Trey sat back and let out a slow breath. "She found other accommodations. Moved out the day I brought Trevor home."

"That's too bad. I mean, Trevor is such a great little boy that I can't imagine any woman wouldn't want to spend time around him."

"Guess it wasn't her thing."

"No women in his life, huh?" She tried for a light tone, yet Trey heard something else in her voice.

"I wouldn't say that. There are two sisters, both widows, who watch him a few hours each day, and a couple of fifteen-year-old twin girls who babysit if one of us isn't back from the base by three o'clock."

"What about when you go out, date?"

"Date? I've had one date since Trevor arrived and that wasn't my doing. I was just helping out a friend."

Connie shook head. "How well I know how much time a baby takes. I don't believe I went out more than four or five times while we had him." She took a deep breath. "Truth is, I wouldn't have had it any other way."

"You miss him."

"Every day. But I know he's where he should be, and I can see you're working hard to provide a loving home. Sydney would be pleased, Trey. I'm certain of it."

They sat in silence for a few moments, watching the activity in the restaurant and listening to the quiet conversations around them.

"You know, you're always welcome to come out for a visit. There's a room we use for guests."

"Maybe someday. Things are a little tight right now." The evasive tone of her voice told Trey there was more involved than a desire to see Trevor. It was the first time it occurred to Trey that Connie might not have the money to make the trip or be able to take time off work.

"We'll make sure it happens, somehow." He held out his glass to hers in a salute, then finished his drink.

"I'd better head home. Tomorrow will be busy." Connie pushed up from her chair. "I am so glad you came. You didn't know Sydney well, but I'm certain she's smiling down at you." She gave Trey one last brief hug, then walked out the door.

He watched her leave, understanding the emptiness she must be feeling at the loss of both her best friend and Trevor. Trey vowed to get her to California for a visit—and soon.

******

It had been a long day and restless night, and now he was packing to catch his plane.

Trey had met a couple of Sydney's distant relatives at the services, but not the ones Mr. Egan had mentioned from up north. Forty or fifty people had been at the church, then everyone formed a procession to the cemetery. Afterwards, they all met at Connie's house.

Trey had taken time to look at the various photos on the wall of Sydney, Connie, and Trevor. One that stood out was of Sydney and Trevor with a good-looking man, who appeared to be in his thirties.

"That's Buddy," Connie said as she walked up behind Trey. "The three of us have been friends for years. You probably didn't notice, but he was at the church and cemetery, but begged off coming here. He'd hit his wall." Connie looked to Trey and saw that he understood.

"Was she seeing anyone?" Trey asked.

"No, not for a few months before she was diagnosed. She dated an attorney a couple of times. It didn't work out." Connie smiled at the memory.

"What's so funny?"

"Truthfully? The guy was a chump. Smart but arrogant."

Trey chuckled. "What about you?" He indicated the people in the room. "Anyone here you've been dating?"

"Nope. I do have my eyes set on someone at the hospital. Poor guy is too busy to notice anyone."

"A doctor, huh?"

"Yeah. There isn't a lot of opportunity when you work as a nurse. There's only so much time in a day, and I'm not much of a partier." She blushed as the words tumbled out of her. "The night you met Sydney was an exception—for both of us." Connie smiled and looked around the room.

"Guess I'd better make the rounds again to be sure I've said spoken with everyone."

Trey grabbed her arm before she left. "I need to take off, Connie." He leaned down to place a kiss on her cheek. "We'll stay in touch."

Connie touched his arm, smiled, then turned toward the others in the room.

Trey watched her for a few more minutes, and vowed, once more, to be sure the woman who'd helped his son's mother would have the opportunity to see Trevor as often as possible.

Chapter Thirteen

"How about six o'clock?" Alex suggested.

Jesse had noticed his business card laying on her dresser a couple of days before, and wondered if the construction company owner was serious about getting together sometime. She'd pondered the possibility a couple of days before, trying to find the courage to pick up the phone and call. He seemed genuinely glad to hear from her. Alex's schedule for breakfast or lunch was full the next several days, so they decided to have a casual dinner at a local hamburger place that evening.

"Sounds great, Alex. I'll see you at six at Bud's." Jesse hung up from the call. That's when she noticed the person next to her. "Hey, Paul."

"Jesse. What's up?"

"Not much." She tried to ignore the fact that he'd overheard the conversation with Alex.

"Sounded like something to me." His narrowed eyes daring her to try to dispute it.

"Not that it's any of your business, but I'm having dinner with a man I met at the dance. That's it."

"Given up on the cowboy, huh?" Paul followed her down the hallway and out the door to the parking lot.

She glanced at her friend and former roommate. "More like he has no interest in trying to work things out with me. I've tried. He pushes me away each time."

"The guy's had a lot on his mind the last few weeks. He's flying back from Pensacola today."

"I knew he was going back for the services."

Paul stopped and turned toward her. "You know, he wasn't with Trevor's mom but one night. It doesn't have anything to do with that, does it?"

"You mean the split?"

"Yep."

"The way I understand it, that night happened before he left for Texas. He and I didn't start going out, at least not as a couple, until a few months before our transfer to California." She fell silent a moment, wondering if there was even a little truth to what Paul said, but shook her head. "No, the split was all about me not knowing how to handle the changes Trevor would bring."

"And now?"

"Now? I'd like an hour alone with Trey to talk things through. At least try to finalize it in my mind, even if he'll never forgive me for taking off like I did." She paused, toying with car keys she held in her hand. "He just isn't interested."

They stopped at Paul's truck. "We're having a barbeque this Saturday. Why don't you come by for a while? Benny and Tony will be there, plus Nate and a few others. I think Reb invited Shelly. What have you got to lose?"

Jesse closed her eyes, wondering if she had enough courage to face Trey once more. "Nothing, I guess. I'll think about it." She turned to head for her Jeep, then looked over her shoulder. "Thanks, Paul."

Jesse drove home, considering the invitation. She had yet to meet Trevor, and even though she could lie to most people, she couldn't deny the truth to herself—there wasn't anything she wanted more than to see Trey.

******

Jesse walked into the small hamburger restaurant to see Alex signaling from a booth near the entrance. He stood as she approached.

"Hi, Jesse. Glad you called." He looked around the packed dining room. "Hope this is okay."

She sat down across the table. "This is great. I've been here several times and it's always good. Of course, I always get the same thing."

"Oh, yeah, and what's that?"

"Burger with blue cheese and bacon, and pickles on the side." She didn't even open her menu.

The waitress walked up and took Jesse's order, then turned to Alex. Jesse watched him as he spoke. He really was a good-looking man. If he weren't still in love with his wife and trying to work things out, any woman would find him a great catch. Every woman, except for her. It had only been a couple of months, yet something inside of Jesse told her it would be a long time before she felt what she did for Trey with another man.

"How are you doing?" Alex sat back in his chair and let the glass of beer roll between his palms.

"Good. We're getting lots of flight time."

"Is your ex also a pilot?"

"Yeah, and a good one. He's with another squadron but also attached to the Reagan. Can't seem to get too far away from him." Jesse tried for a smile, yet it didn't quite reach her eyes.

"Must be tough—working around him, I mean." Alex looked up as the waitress set down their food then left. He inhaled deeply. "Ah, that smells great."

Jesse wasted no time digging into the meal. Juice dripped down her fingers as she bit into the messy burger. "They sure do a great job on their burgers." She grinned and grabbed for a napkin.

"Yeah, they do." Alex snatched a couple of fries. "So is it tough, working together?"

Jesse set down her burger and wiped the juice from her hands. "Not really, at least not as tough as it could be if we were in the same squadron. I don't see him every day. What about you? Any word from your wife?"

"I got a call yesterday." A tentative smile crossed his face. "She's flying out this weekend. Wants to talk things over, try to work it out."

"That is great news. You must be thrilled."

"Yes and no. I'm trying not to read too much into it. I flew back to Texas a few months ago, hoping to do the same thing, but she wasn't interested—wanted me to move back and let Mike take over the company. Now she talks as if she's

119

ready to come back to California." He finished his meal and sat back. "We'll see."

The two relaxed and talked about her flying, then shifted to his projects at the base and plans for his own home. The drawings were complete, but the house had never been started. His wife leaving had put a stop to everything.

"Must be exciting to build your own place. I wouldn't even know where to begin." Jesse sipped her beer, realizing she was glad she'd made the call to Alex. It was good to get out with someone whose life wasn't wrapped up in flying.

"Oh, I believe you'd handle it just fine. All you do is list what you want, set a budget, and start sketching out what you'd like. It's not as hard as some people make it out to be."

Jesse looked up at the sound of a child's laughter coming through the door, and her heart stopped. Trey walked in carrying his son, followed by Reb and Paul. *Damn him*, Jesse thought and narrowed her eyes at her squadron partner. This was no random encounter. At least Paul had the good sense to avoid eye contact.

"Well, hi there, Jesse." Reb clapped her shoulder and held out his hand to Alex. "Don't think we've met. Ryan Cantrell, but most people call me Reb."

Alex stood and accepted the outstretched hand. "Alex Parker." He introduced himself to Paul and Trey. "And who's this little guy?"

Trey had walked into the restaurant unaware that Paul had set him up. He didn't suspect a thing, even as his eyes zeroed in on Jesse and the man at her table. Trey recognized him as the same man he'd seen her with at the dance—the man Jesse had said she'd just met. He wasn't prepared for the punch to his gut that seeing Jesse with another man triggered.

"This is my son, Trevor," Trey replied without breaking eye contact with Jesse.

She squirmed under his gaze and tried to look away. Her eyes finally shifted to Trevor, and her heart kicked a little at how much the young boy resembled his father.

She reached out a hand and stroked the boy's arm. "Hello, Trevor. I'm Jesse."

He looked at her and Alex, wide-eyed, before tightening his arms around Trey and resting his head on his father's shoulder.

Trey shifted Trevor to his other side. "You'll have to excuse him. He didn't get a nap, and it's been a long day." Again, his eyes focused on Jesse as if daring her to acknowledge him.

Jesse moistened her lips, allowing only three words to escape. "He's gorgeous, Trey."

Alex watched the intense reaction Jesse had to the man he'd just met. It didn't take a genius to figure out who he was. "You three work with Jesse on base?" His question was directed to Trey.

"Yes," Trey replied, not shifting his gaze.

Reb watched for a moment before stepping in. "Good to meet you, Alex. See you on base, Jesse." He nudged Trey's arm, indicating it was time to move on.

Alex sat back down, placed his elbows on the table, and clasped his hands. "So, that's him?"

Jesse's eyes widened for an instant before she looked down at her empty plate. "That's the one."

"You never mentioned he had a kid."

"Trey just learned of Trevor not long before we split up," she answered with staid calmness. "It's complicated."

"You know what? You've been great about listening to me, now it's my turn. Fire away."

Jesse didn't know where the words came from, but over the course of another thirty minutes, she filled Alex in on the relationship and break up. Shelly was the one other person who'd been a sounding board. Talking about everything one more time helped settle in her mind how far apart she and Trey were as well as how unlikely it would be to work things out. She ached each time the memories of the last few weeks surfaced, knowing her mistake might never be righted.

"What's your plan now?" Alex asked as he drained the last of his beer.

"Now?" Jesse's puzzled expression wasn't lost on Alex.

He chuckled at her confusion. "It's obvious the two of you still have feelings for each other. I just met the guy and it was clear to me. The question is, what are you going to do about it?"

Jesse took a breath, pondering Alex's question, and wondering if she might be giving up too soon. "I've attempted twice to speak with him, apologize, and explain. He turned me away each time. Trey is a good man, stubborn, but fair. And proud. Why would he trust me to not do the same thing again?"

"You mean not embracing the role of being a mom without thinking it through?" A probing query came into his eyes.

"I've never quite thought of it that way, but yes. I know my life must seem simple to most. I fly, go to the gym, eat, rest, then get up and fly again. Add to that my relationship with Trey and my life seemed full, yet with too many unknowns."

"Unknowns?"

"Such as would we always be stationed at the same base? Even though our squadrons are assigned to carriers based at Coronado that might not always be the case. That could mean one might be on deployment to Asia while the other is in the Middle East. How many relationships survive these types of challenges?"

Alex crossed his arms, considering her concerns, yet felt she was still throwing too much away. "You got into the Academy when the odds were against you. You earned a spot in pilot training, and I assume the odds were against you then also. Now you fly jets, a tough job in a world dominated by men. You've been successful through it all. Do you really believe you wouldn't be successful at working out the challenges married pilots face?"

"Married?" she squeaked out. "I never mentioned marriage."

"You didn't have to. No one goes through this much angst over saving or discarding a relationship unless they're considering the long haul. Are you saying you two never discussed getting married?"

She took a deep breath and exhaled slowly. "Sure, we discussed it a few times."

"I'm no family counselor—hell, I haven't been able to save my own marriage—yet. In my book, the two of you have something worth salvaging. You just need to decide how much work and pain you're willing to endure before he comes to his senses and lets you back inside." Alex checked his watch. "Guess I'd better get going. My wife is flying in tomorrow night and I have some serious house cleaning to do."

Jesse followed him outside feeling as if she'd gone through a brief therapy session. The thing was, everything Alex said made complete sense. "Thanks. I didn't mean for this to be a help Jesse dinner."

"Are you kidding? It was a nice change to talk about something other than building permits and budget issues." He drew Jesse into a brief hug. "Hang in there. It's my guess it'll be worth it."

******

Trey sat inside, watching the intense conversation going on between Jesse and the new man, Alex. He figured they must have something truly important to discuss by the looks on both of their faces. He'd been about ready to hand Trevor off to one of the guys and march over to her table when they'd stood to walk outside. A moment later he watched as Alex pulled Jesse into a hug. Good thing the guy hadn't kissed her as that might have been more than Trey could handle.

"What are you going to do about them?" Paul asked as he finished his burger and nodded in the direction of the parking lot.

A light came on in Trey's head. "You dirt bag. You knew she'd be here, with him, right?"

"Let's just say I had an inkling of it."

"Down, Dada," Trevor demanded as he stuffed one more small french fry into his mouth. Trey grabbed more napkins and wiped off his son's face and hands, then watched him climb off the seat.

"You stay right here, Trevor. You understand?"

Trevor bobbed his head several times before turning to run down the aisle. Reb was quick and reached out his arm to stop him. "Well, that worked out well," Reb said as he scooped Trev up into his arms. "Maybe it's time to head out."

Trey stood and reached out to take his son, but Reb ignored him.

"Hey, I've been gone a couple of days. Hand my son over."

Reb whispered in Trevor's ear. "You want to go with your daddy or stay with Uncle Reb?"

"Web," Trevor giggled as he squirmed to be put back down.

"Oh, that's just great," Trey grumbled as he fished for a tip in his pockets, threw it on the table, and followed the others out. He watched Trevor scramble toward the door and thought about how his life had changed over the last four months. Who would've thought he'd be busier than ever, feeling more needed while at the same time holding a gut-wrenching emptiness inside? Life just didn't make sense.

Chapter Fourteen

Trey had finished the flight exercises for the day and was making his way from the tarmac to the debrief meeting. It had been a long day after a difficult week and Trey was glad it was almost over—he was looking forward to the weekend.

"Hey, wait up."

Trey turned back to see Reb and Paul walking up to him.

"Mind if we stop and grab some stuff for the barbeque tomorrow?" Reb pulled a list from his back pocket.

"Not a problem," Trey replied as he stepped into the truck and started the engine.

Fifteen minutes later he followed Reb and Paul around the store, pushing a cart almost full of groceries. He kept watching as Reb threw more stuff into the basket. "How many people are coming, anyway?"

"Don't know, maybe thirty."

"Thirty? I thought this was just a small get-together. You know, some R and R time, laughs, relax."

Reb turned toward him and shrugged. "What can I say? People love our parties." He smiled then glanced down at his list. "That's it."

"Our three squadrons, right?" Trey asked as they loaded bags into the back seat.

"And a few other strays. Not to worry. If it gets to be too much for you, feel free to grab Trevor and take off," Reb joked, then sobered. "You know, Jesse is planning to come for a while."

Trey took that in, surprised that it hadn't already occurred to him that she might be included. "She bringing anyone with her?"

"Don't know. Last I knew she was flying solo," Paul answered.

Trey slammed the transmission into drive and peeled out of the lot. All he could picture was Jesse and her friend, Alex, last night at Bub's, with their heads together, talking.

"Hey, man, settle down. This truck doesn't have the same kind of warranty as the jets." Reb tightened his seat belt then laid his arm across the seat back. "Even if she brings someone, so what? You've decided to move on, right?"

Trey pursed his lips. "Right," he mumbled and focused on the road ahead. He knew Reb was wrong in his assessment that he'd moved on. Trey felt he'd just gone through the motions much of the time over the last few weeks, being a dad, flying, attending Sydney's funeral. They may have filled his time, but not his life or his heart. Maybe tomorrow he could start to turn that around.

******

"Show me to the beer," someone shouted when they stepped onto the back patio where the music was blaring and the barbeque smoked.

Trey didn't turn his gaze from the burgers on the grill, just pointed toward the coolers that held soda, water, and beer. He'd been standing in that same spot for a while, watching the happenings while keeping an eye on Trevor who played with a couple of other toddlers in the grass area beside him.

His mind wandered to the quick message he'd gotten off to Connie the night before. A message and flight information. She'd responded almost immediately with an affirmative, and he now waited for the phone call that would take him to the small airport that wasn't far away. She'd been able to get Monday and Tuesday off, which would give her almost three days with Trevor. He felt good about taking the step to get her to California. He felt the phone in his pocket vibrate.

"Yeah? Hey, Connie." Trey waited a moment. "Sure. Give me twenty minutes tops." He slid the phone back into his pocket. "Reb!" he shouted over the elevating noise level.

"Need more burgers?" Reb asked as he stepped over folding chairs and toys on his way to the grill.

"I need to pick someone up at the airport. Take over for me." He handed the spatula over, grabbed Trevor, and was out the door before Reb could say another word.

"What's up with Trey?" Paul popped the top off a beer and handed it to Reb.

"Says he needs to pick somebody up at the airport. That's all I know."

It wasn't five minutes before the two looked up to see Jesse walk outside followed by Benny and Tony. "Jesse," Paul called. "Over here."

"Great party, boys." Jesse gave each a quick hug before grabbing a drink and walking back to stand near the grill. She looked around, disappointment clear on her face.

"He'll be back," Reb said.

"Who?" she asked, hoping it wasn't obvious that she'd been looking for Trey.

He narrowed his eyes at her, not taking the bait. "He left to pick someone up from the airport." Reb watched her glance at the children. "Took Trevor with him."

"You know, I'd never seen Trey's son until the other night at Bud's. It's amazing how much Trevor already looks like his dad."

"He's a great father. Of course, Trev prefers his two uncles," Paul interjected and placed an arm across Reb's shoulders. Both men smiled at Jesse, who laughed and turned to walk away.

That's when she saw them—Trey and a beautiful woman with golden blond hair that fell to her shoulders. She was holding Trevor who had his arms wound tight around her neck. Jesse's heart slammed into her chest at the look Trey gave the woman as he escorted her outside. He had his hand on the small of her back and leaned in to whisper something. Her laughter pealed through the crowd. The two of them made a stunning couple, even in jeans and t-shirts.

"Wow," Paul said and started walking toward Trey.

"I'll be damned. Wonder who she is?" Reb flipped burgers while trying to keep his eyes on the woman with Trey.

Trey walked a few feet onto the patio and stopped. "Everyone, this is Connie."

Most raised their glasses or cans to acknowledge the new arrival, while others, like Paul, made a beeline toward her.

"Connie, this is one of my roommates, Paul Henshaw. My other roommate, Reb, is tending the barbeque. You'll have to put up with both of them while you're here."

Connie smiled at Paul and held out her hand. "Oh, I think I can manage that."

"Here," Paul said. "Let me take Trevor and I'll introduce you around." Trev turned at the sound of Paul's voice and reached out his arms. "He'll probably just want down within a couple of seconds." They turned toward a group of people, leaving Trey alone.

He'd seen Jesse right off, as soon as he'd stepped outside with Connie. She'd remained rooted in place making no attempt to acknowledge either of them. His eyes remained fixed on her. She'd stepped back toward Reb, focusing on the burgers, then turning her back toward Trey in a blatant attempt to ignore him. From what he could tell she'd come alone.

"Hello, Jesse."

She hadn't seen him come up behind her. All Jesse wanted was to stay for a little longer then disappear. Maybe take a run, go to the gym or for groceries, anything except watch Trey with his pretty guest.

"Hello, Trey. Nice party." Jesse took a long swallow of her beer, then decided to finish it off before tossing the empty can in the recycle bin.

"It's pretty much all Reb and Paul's doing. I just try to keep up."

"Who's the woman?" Reb asked.

"A friend of Sydney's. Take another look, Reb. You might remember her."

Reb removed his sunglasses and took a closer look. "Oh, yeah. The sexy blond who wouldn't give me the time of day." He turned to Jesse. "Completely shunned me. Really messed with my ego for months."

Jesse couldn't contain the smile that split her face. There wasn't a single bachelor pilot with a bigger ego, at least about women, than Reb.

"Anyway, it seemed like a good idea to fly her out. Let her spend some time with Trev." Trey continued to watch Jesse, trying to figure a way to get her alone and talk. "She'll stay in Trevor's room. Flies out on Tuesday."

"Good. That'll give me some time to work my magic on her. Unless of course, you have first rights." Reb picked up one burger after another and placed them on a serving plate. "Here, pass these around." He shoved the plate at Jesse, who grabbed it like a lifeline and walked away. "What the hell were you thinking?" Reb asked when Jesse was a good distance away.

"What are you talking about?" Trey was baffled at Reb's question.

"Don't mess with me, okay? You're still not close to being your usual self—haven't been since Jesse moved out. There's so much tension whenever the two of you are close you'd think an earthquake was about to hit." He looked up to see Jesse talking with a group of fellow pilots. "She's still in love with you, you know."

"I still don't get what's eating at you." Trey wasn't connecting any dots on this one.

"Connie, dumbass. Is she with you or just here to visit Trevor? From where I stand, it looks as if she's your new lady."

A light went on in Trey's head. "Ah, hell," he murmured.

"Just as I thought." Reb gave him a pointed look. "If you want Jesse back, and it's pretty clear you do, you'd better do some damage control now before that hole gets any deeper."

Both remained quiet—Reb concentrating on the grill, and Trey trying to figure a way to talk himself out of this one. It was an easy explanation, yet with Connie staying at the house, he was afraid Jesse wouldn't see it that way.

"What are you two so quiet about?"

Reb glanced up to see Shelly standing a couple of feet away, looking great in white shorts and a halter top. They hadn't connected as planned after the dance last weekend, and his body was telling him it had been too long. He handed the spatula to Trey and drew Shelly into a hug.

"Glad you could make it, baby. Do not even think of leaving without me," he whispered as she stepped back.

"Wouldn't think of it." Shelly smiled before leaving Reb to search out Jesse.

"Damn, she's a fine looking woman," Reb grumbled as he watched her hips swaying and her laughing at something someone had said.

"And that's a problem?" Trey asked, keeping his eye on Jesse. He wasn't going to let her take off before they spoke.

"Yeah, a big problem." Reb and Shelly had started out casual, each knowing it was just a short-term thing, something to fill the time for each of them. His feelings for her had grown until he knew he'd either have to stop seeing Shelly or ramp things up, assuming she felt the same. It was damned inconvenient and unexpected.

Trey took a long look at his friend and, realizing he was serious, clapped his hand on Reb's shoulder. "Happens to us all, my man." He strolled over to the cooler and grabbed a water, twisted off the cap, and drank half the bottle. Jesse was talking with Shelly, surrounded by other women, all laughing. Paul was still introducing Connie to everyone while holding Trevor's hand.

"Trey," someone yelled from the other side of the good-sized backyard and waved him over.

Trey took one more look at Jesse then made his way through lounge chairs, coolers, and kids to the group by the back fence. "How are you doing, Pete?" Pete's wife, Anita, also a pilot, was stationed on the east coast. Trey had talked to him once about how it was working, being stationed thousands of miles apart. His friend had told him it was tough but workable. It all depended on how committed you were to each other as well as the trust factor. Not long afterwards Trey had learned about Trevor and Jesse had moved out. Jesse and he didn't appear to have built either.

"Great. Still hoping to get Anita transferred out here. We'll just keep at it until it happens." Pete was the most positive person Trey had ever met and an excellent pilot. He was the kind of man you wanted as your friend. "Who's that with Paul?"

Trey explained the relationship between Connie and Trevor. He was glad he no longer had to explain his instant fatherhood—everyone had met his son and treated him as if he'd been with Trey all along.

"Sure seems like Paul has taken a liking to her. Interesting," Pete commented before he stood to meet Connie as Paul walked up to them.

Paul introduced Connie to the group as Trey took Trevor's hand then picked up his son to walk toward Jesse.

"I don't know if you've had a chance to get to know Trevor." Trey stood next to her, turning his son around so that Trevor faced Jesse.

Jesse pulled her surprised gaze from Trey to the little boy who stared at her. "No, I haven't had much time with him." Jesse reached out to touch Trevor's hand. He watched her but didn't turn away.

"Is it okay if Jesse watches you for a while, son?" Trey set Trevor on the ground and watched him run toward the other children a few yards away. "Do you mind keeping track of him while I help Reb?"

Her chest tightened at his gesture. "Yes, I'd like that very much."

Trey started toward the grill, turning his back on Jesse, letting her know Trevor was all hers. He knew he could watch them while he finished the last of the burgers, and preferred to let them get acquainted without his presence. For Trey, this was the first step.

Chapter Fifteen

Connie and Jesse sat in the living room watching as Trevor rolled his ball around. This lasted for about two minutes before he searched for some other toy to occupy his time.

"He's gotten so big." Connie leaned over to toss a new toy in Trevor's direction. "There are times when it feels as if the time has flown since Trey brought him out here and at other times the days just drag. Those are the days I dread the most."

"It must have been hard losing both Trevor and his mother within a few weeks. I can't imagine going through it." Jesse looked over her shoulder when she heard laughter coming from the kitchen. The party had ended an hour before, and Trey had asked her to stay to keep Connie company while the men cleaned up.

She still wasn't sure of Connie's relationship with Trey. Perhaps this would give her a chance to figure it out. Even though Jesse had come to terms with the fact that it was over and she needed to move on, a part of her prayed that Trey would reach out to her, try to repair their broken relationship.

"My nursing job keeps me pretty busy. I volunteer at a community center once a week and I'm thinking of taking a cooking class. You know, one of those gourmet things." She tried for a smile, but Jesse could see the sadness in Connie's eyes.

"Do you have any time to go out, date?" Jesse tried for nonchalance hoping Connie didn't figure out the real reason for her curiosity.

Connie gave a short laugh and slid onto the carpeted floor to play with Trevor. "I went out a couple of times with someone several months ago. A nice guy, smart, doing well, but, I don't know, there just isn't any zing with him." She looked up and over her shoulder at Jesse. "Don't you think there should be some type of spark?"

Jesse thought about it.

She'd been attracted to Trey from their first meeting at the Academy, yet kept her feelings to herself, not wanting anyone, least of all Trey, to know. Jesse had been stunned when he'd asked her out on a date. She'd learned that he'd felt the same all those years but had never said a word. Their first kiss sent a jolt through her body that only increased each time they were together. If that was a spark, then yes, they'd had it.

"Yes, I do think there must be chemistry. Perhaps you'll meet someone this weekend." When Connie smiled and shook her head, Jesse continued. "I'm serious. There are a lot of good-looking, great guys around here and most are single. You never know." Jesse smiled and slid onto the floor beside Connie.

"Well, there is someone I met today. He's the first man in a long time who has caught my attention. I felt an instant rapport with him, if you know what I mean."

"Paul?"

Connie's stunned expression told Jesse she'd guessed right.

"Don't worry, he won't hear it from me. I've known Paul a long time, and he's the best. Can get a little grumpy, but I love him—in a buddy way, I mean," Jesse corrected before they both started to laugh. That brought Trey out of the kitchen, along with Shelly, who'd stayed behind to help, or supervise as Reb labeled it.

"What's going on?" Trey's eyes roamed the room, looking at the pile of toys and the women sitting close together on the floor.

"Not a lot, just talking and watching Trevor." Jesse pushed herself up then reached into her pocket for the Jeep keys. "Guess I'd better head out."

Connie stood up as well and gave Jesse a hug. "I'm so glad we had a chance to talk. Maybe I'll see you again before I leave on Tuesday."

"I'm running at six tomorrow morning. Why don't you join me?" Jesse suggested.

"Run?" The look on Connie's face had them all laughing.

"I'm taking Connie to the steakhouse tomorrow with Paul, Reb, and Shelly. Why don't you join us?" Trey moved the short distance to stand next to Jesse. He was close enough to smell her shampoo and sense the tension in her body.

"Good idea," Paul added. "Get away from the boneheads you live with for a night."

"I don't remember you calling them that when you came over last week for Tony's lasagna."

"It was a lapse." Paul grinned. "Seriously, come with us."

Jesse looked at Trey. "That might work." She kept her voice even in an attempt to hide the excitement she felt at his invitation. Expecting this to be some grand turnaround was too much, yet she couldn't stop herself from hoping.

"Come on. I'll walk you out." Trey opened the door and followed Jesse to her Jeep. "I'm glad you came today." He shoved his hands in his pockets, but he couldn't stop his eyes from locking on hers, searching for anything that would tip him off as to what she was feeling. Being close to her was too much of a temptation and he didn't want to blow the fragile connection that had begun.

She didn't retreat into the safety of the Jeep, choosing instead to keep the short distance between his body and hers—just enough space where each could feel the attraction tempt them. Jesse wanted to reach up, cup his cheek, and run her fingers over the dark stubble that had begun.

"I'm glad I came too."

Her tentative smile was too much for Trey. Maybe he was reading too much into it, but perhaps he wasn't. He raised a hand to her face, caressing it with a finger, then tilted her chin up. He placed a quick, soft kiss on her lips, then stepped back.

"Tomorrow at the steakhouse." His voice had grown rough, even from that one brief encounter.

"I'll be there." This time Jesse did seek the barrier of her Jeep, started the engine and pulled away. She looked in the mirror to see Trey still standing at the curb, watching as she increased the distance between them.

Jesse looked at the steering wheel and saw her hands shaking. She gripped the wheel tighter and took a deep breath. Once more she cautioned herself not to read too much into the simple kiss, yet her body still vibrated from the touch, and she couldn't stop the hope in her heart or the fear which accompanied it.

******

Her morning run was long and brutal—by design. Jesse needed to clear her head and get a grip on her raging emotions. She hadn't slept for more than a couple of hours and felt the lack of sleep with each step.

Jesse had chosen to run along the Kings River. There were a few fishermen out, seeking bass and enjoying what was turning into a beautiful morning. She kept promising herself to rent a small boat with gear and go out on the river, yet it still sat on her list of to-do items, ignored and pretty much forgotten—except when she'd go on a run. Jesse had grown up on the bayou, fishing for redfish or whatever she could get. It had been a lot of years since she'd taken a rod and reel in her hand and experienced the peaceful feeling of sitting in a boat while she waited for a bite. Next weekend, she told herself, knowing she mentally promised herself the same thing each time she drove to the river.

She made a turn and headed back to her Jeep waving to some of the fishermen as she ran past. Jesse looked up at the sound of the small, private jet that flew overhead. It reminded her of the MacLaren plane and their trip to Fire Mountain. It had been one of the best weekends she'd had in a long time, and she remembered the anticipation she felt at the prospect of returning. So much had happened since then. Jesse wondered if she'd ever see the ranch, and Trey's family, again.

******

"That's it, Trevor. Great job, son." Trey had Trevor in the backyard pool where Marissa and Miranda lived. He'd asked them to watch Trevor that night while the adults went to dinner, and the request had turned into an invitation for everyone to join them at their pool. It was the twins' family, Trey, Trevor, Connie, and Paul. Trey had been surprised when Paul had accepted—he wasn't one for socializing with the neighbors. This time, however, there was Connie to encourage him—and it hadn't taken much. Reb and Shelly had plans, but Shelly had found a swimsuit she thought would fit Connie and brought it over.

"Do it again, Mr. MacLaren. I want to get a picture," Marissa called as she lifted her cell phone to her face.

"Okay, Trevor, you ready?" When his son smiled, Trey blew a soft breath into Trevor's face, which caused the toddler to suck in a breath and close his eyes. Trey held tight and dunked his son into the water then pulled him back up after a couple of seconds. Trevor popped up, rubbing his eyes and giggling as Trey pulled him close.

"Is he taking lessons?" Connie asked from her seat on a lounge chair next to Paul.

"Not yet. He starts in a couple of weeks. I had no idea you had to sign up weeks, sometimes months, in advance for that stuff." Trey was still learning the ropes of being a single dad and the pre-planning that went with it. "Trevor's schedule takes as much planning as my flying," Trey joked.

"Is it tough for you?" Paul asked Connie who sat next to him, eating chips and watching the actions in the pool.

"Not being near Trevor?" Connie asked. At Paul's nod, she continued. "Yes, it's hard. I love him like he was mine. I was in the birthing room with Sydney, by her side, the whole time. I'm primarily an emergency room and trauma nurse. I was involved in quite a number of deliveries during my training. Yet, this one was special. I knew Trevor would be a part of my life forever, or at least that's what I'd thought at the time." She let out a deep breath and shifted her gaze to the pool. "Guess you never know, huh?"

"It was good that Trey brought you out." Paul didn't say more. He'd been attracted to Connie the moment Trey had introduced her. In all his years, he'd never felt such an immediate connection to someone. He had two days to try to make something work—what that was, he didn't know, but there was an attraction between them he wanted to explore.

"I've actually had thoughts of trying to get a job out here to be closer to him."

Paul liked that idea. "That sounds like a fine idea to me."

She glanced at him, surprised at his quick response. "I don't know. It's a big move. Plus, what happens when Trey is transferred or marries? It might be that his wife won't want someone like me being around."

Paul thought of what he'd seen in the front yard last night between Trey and Jesse. He'd been about ready to meet a couple of buddies at a bar not far away, when he'd almost interrupted what appeared to be the first step in a reconciliation. If that was the case, Paul was certain Jessie wouldn't have any issue with Connie living nearby.

"You have a couple of days to decide if it's an idea worth pursuing. In the meantime, relax, don't worry your time away."

Connie laughed and glanced over at Paul.

"What so funny?" His gaze shot to hers.

"That's what my grandmother used to say, and just like that. 'Don't worry your time away, Connie,' she used to tell me whenever I'd stress out."

Paul chuckled, remembering his aunt up in Montana. "My aunt used to say it to me any time she realized I was at a crossroads. It was one of her favorite expressions."

"What kind of crossroads?"

"I struggled with accepting the appointment to the Naval Academy. My family lived in Missoula, Montana, and my uncle and aunt owned a ranch about an hour away. I spent a lot of time there on school breaks. My parents had me pretty late in life—they're in their sixties now. I struggled with being at school all the way across the country." He hadn't thought about the decision for years. At the time, it had consumed his thoughts, causing him to miss sleep and almost walk away from a great opportunity.

"But you accepted. Was it the right decision?"

"Absolutely. No regrets and my parents are still doing well. Guess you have to take a chance sometimes." Paul laid back in the lounge chair, rested his hand behind his head, and closed his eyes. The sun felt good. Being with Connie felt great. He needed to think through some things quickly and decide what he wanted to do about the woman who sat beside him.

"You two ready to head back?" Trey stood next to Paul, holding Trevor. Both were dripping wet.

Connie grabbed a towel and reached out to Trevor, who went into her arms without hesitation. She dried him off, dressed him in shorts and a t-shirt, and was ready to head out within a couple of minutes. Both men watched in awe at her efficient movements.

She set Trevor down, took his hand, and looked at the two men. "You guys ready?"

"Yes, ma'am." Paul's mouth turned up at the corners as he grabbed his towel and shirt.

They thanked the twins and their parents for inviting them before walking out the side gate. Connie let go of Trevor's hand and let him run up the sidewalk and onto the neighbor's lawn. At almost seventeen months, he was running most of the time, exploring everything, and forming new words. It all moved fast.

"I'm going to put Trevor down for his nap, then crash for a while." Trey threw the wet clothes and towels on the washer and headed upstairs before calling over his shoulder, "We'll leave for dinner at six."

Paul stood next to Connie wondering how to get her out for a while.

"Hungry?"

"Famished," Connie replied.

"Great. Let's change and go find something."

Twenty minutes later, Paul knocked on Trey's door and pulled it open. "Connie and I are going to get some food. You want anything?"

Trey sat against the headboard of his bed, a book in his lap, and tried to keep from nodding off. Even with the baby monitor on the table, he still felt uncomfortable relying on it to notify him when Trevor woke up. "No, I'm good."

Paul closed the door. Trey could hear his friend's truck start up and pull away.

He thought of Jesse and wondered what she was doing. He reached for his cell phone, almost reconsidered, then punched her number in speed dial.

"Hey," she answered on the third ring.

"Hey, yourself." His stomach did a flip at the sound of her voice. He needed to say something, but his mind went blank.

"Trey, you there?"

"Uh, yeah." A slight panic dashed through him as he struggled for something to say. "Just got back from the pool with Paul and Connie. They took off to get food, and, well, I felt like calling."

Jesse's heart had skipped a beat when she'd looked at her caller ID and saw it was Trey. Her first thought was that he'd changed his mind about inviting her to dinner, and she'd held her breath. Her relief at hearing his words was tangible.

"I'm glad you did." Her words were soft and drifted between them.

"What have you been doing today?" Trey cringed. It was no longer his right to ask.

"I went for a run along the river, picked up a sandwich from that little place we like, then came home and started laundry. Pretty exciting, huh?"

"Excitement is way overrated."

"Agreed. What are you doing?" Jesse took a seat on a dining room chair and rested her elbows on the table.

"Trevor's down for a nap, so I'm trying to read. Couldn't concentrate."

"Probably tired."

"Among other stuff." Trey paused for a moment. "I miss you, Jesse."

Jesse sat up in the chair and ran a hand through her short hair. She let out a breath before answering. "I miss you too."

He wasn't sure how to proceed, yet Trey knew he couldn't leave the conversation hanging. "I want to try to work things out."

Jesse didn't hesitate. "So do I."

"Come back to the house after dinner. I'll put Trevor down, make sure Paul or Connie can keep watch, and we'll take a walk—see what happens."

"All right. That sounds good."

"I'll see you at the steak house tonight."

"See you then." Jesse hit the end button and set the phone on the table. She blinked a few times, stopping the tears before they could fall, and hoped whatever happened tonight would be a new start for them.

Chapter Sixteen

Everyone had a great time at the steakhouse. The food was good, and for a Sunday, the place was packed. Connie had sat on one side of Trevor, with Paul next to her. A couple of hours later they drove back to the house. Paul had no problem staying at the house with Connie. He grabbed a movie and settled down next to her on the sofa while Trey and Jesse walked out the front door.

"Thanks again for dinner," Jesse said as she and Trey started down the sidewalk at a slow pace.

"Glad you were able to come." Trey reached over to grab her hand and lace his fingers through hers. "I'm sorry I didn't give you a chance to explain why you needed to move out. I've regretted it ever since. Couldn't get myself to move past the thought that you were walking away."

She glanced over at him and squeezed his fingers in hers. "That was my fault. I botched it up, made a mess of things." She swallowed, then licked her lips. "My concern was about what would happen if Trevor got used to me being around and then we split up. I was afraid of Trevor's reaction, but also my own. I knew I'd lose two people, not just one, and I got scared. Can you understand?"

"I suppose so." He stopped and turned her toward him, grasping both her hands in his. "You've known for a long time how I feel about you. I love you, Jesse, and would marry you tomorrow if you were ready." He stopped to swipe away a tear that began to trail down her cheek. "We both have concerns about two pilots marrying, and now there's Trevor. I don't know how everything would work, yet I don't want to lose you because of the unknown. We're two strong, smart people. We can figure this out."

Jesse's heart pounded an incessant rhythm and she felt a surge of excitement at hearing his words. "It would be hard, Trey, facing more obstacles than most couples. The stress and long-distance assignments would be brutal and could pull us apart. The truth is I don't want to go through the same type of pain I've experienced the last couple of months. Not being with you has been torture."

Trey pulled her to him, wrapped his arms around her, and stroked her hair. "The difference would be that we would have committed ourselves to each other. If we love and trust each other, we can make it through the next few years. After that, we have all kinds of choices ahead of us." He closed his eyes and rested his chin on the top of her head.

She pulled him tight, then stepped back and looked up into his bright, clear blue eyes. "I love you and want to work this out. Can we take it a day at a time for a while, get used to being back together, and let me get to know Trevor?"

It all sounded reasonable. "How much time do you need?" Trey leaned down and placed a kiss on her forehead, then one on the corner of each eye before trailing kisses down her cheek and capturing her mouth. She rested her hands on his shoulders before moving them up around his neck.

He moved a hand into her hair and held her to him, deepening the kiss for a brief moment before pulling back and resting his forehead against hers.

"How much time, Jesse?" His voice was husky and his eyes had turned a deep, midnight blue.

"Not long. Just until we're both certain." She prayed he would agree.

"All right. But we'll see each other as often as we can. Agreed?"

"Yes." She brushed another kiss across his firm, warm lips, feeling relief, excitement, and fear all at the same time.

Jesse knew she could work through it all. She loved him and accepted that Trey would do all in his power to make the marriage work. She'd do the same. Jesse just needed a little time to get past her fear of failing and her pain from the last few weeks.

******

While Trey and Jesse were out, Paul briefly explained their history to Connie. She'd known Trey had recently split with someone, but it was a surprise that the woman was Jesse.

"When you see them together, they do seem perfect for each other," Connie commented when Paul had finished.

"They are. I truly hope it works out for them." They still sat on the sofa. Paul had an arm around

151

Connie and pulled her to him. When she looked up, he leaned down and placed a kiss on her full, soft lips, gently gliding over then increasing the pressure before pulling back and staring into her eyes. She winced at the confusion she saw on his face.

"That bad, huh?" She offered a tentative smile.

"No. That good."

He claimed her mouth again with his, and each felt the same sensations race through their bodies as with the first touch of their lips. They deepened the kiss while tightening their hold on each other until they were forced to stop from lack of air. "Good Lord, lady. You can kiss," Paul breathed against her mouth.

"So can you." Connie's heart raced at the impact of their kiss. She couldn't remember a time when it had seemed so perfect.

Paul reached for her again before the sound of the front door opening stopped him. He gave Connie a look of regret, then pulled away and stood. Trey and Jesse walked in, holding hands, looking as they had before the split. His eyes lowered to Connie, who still sat on the sofa, hands in her lap, trying to look as if nothing had happened.

"Good walk?" Paul asked, his voice husky.

Jesse looked from him to Connie and realized she and Trey had interrupted something. She mouthed, *sorry,* to which Paul just shrugged.

"Yeah. It was a great walk. Thanks for watching Trevor. Did he wake up?"

"Not a peep. We checked a couple of times and he didn't stir." Connie pushed herself from the sofa and stood next to Paul. She could still feel the electricity flow between them. "I guess I'd better head upstairs. You know, still trying to adjust to west coast time. I'm looking forward to being with Trevor while you guys are at work. Well, uh, goodnight." She took the stairs two at a time, then closed the bedroom door behind her.

Trey looked at Paul. "What did you do to her? She dashed out of here like a scared rabbit."

"Nothing, bro. Guess she was just tired." Paul winked at Jesse. "See you on base, Jesse." Paul followed Connie upstairs wishing he could detour into her room and not head straight to his.

"What was that all about?" Trey turned a puzzled look at Jesse.

"If I were to guess, I think we have a budding romance on our hands." Jesse grinned and tightened her grip on his hand.

"No, kidding? Well, I'll be damned." Trey dragged a hand through his already mussed hair then pulled Jesse to him. "We'll work through this. You can bet on it."

******

"What's going on?" Trey asked as he walked into a large operations room where most of the pilots had congregated. It was Monday afternoon and the squadrons were returning from their exercises.

"We're not sure, but it seems that Pete had problems and may have had to bail."

"Where?"

"Over the Sierras, we think. We're all waiting for more information."

"SAR is up," someone yelled, and the group walked out to see two search and rescue helicopters take off in the direction of the Sierra Nevada mountain range.

"Commander's inside," one of the men shouted from the doorway, and all of the pilots returned to the large room.

That's when Trey saw Jesse, standing against the back wall, her eyes focused on the officer standing at the front. He walked over to her and stood so that their arms touched, then waited.

"A plane is down in the Sierras. The pilot, Pete Baker, ejected. Two helos have been sent out to find him. We have no word on his condition at this time. Any questions?"

"Do you know why he ejected?" someone called out.

"There aren't many details at this time. His squadron is coming in now. I should have more information within the hour. You may stay here or head out and check back. It's up to you. Any other questions?" No one spoke. The officer walked back through the exit doors. The room fell silent and no one moved. It was clear everyone would stay until they knew more about Pete.

"Jesus," Reb said as he and Paul walked up to Trey and Jesse.

Jesse turned her gaze to Trey. "I don't know the protocol for this. Should I text Anita or will command get in touch with her?"

"Hold on, I'll find out." Trey dashed through the door where the officer had exited and was back a few minutes later. "Don't do anything. Command will notify Anita and make arrangements to get her out here if needed."

"Okay." Jesse felt adrift, as if she should be doing something, helping. The reality was all they could do was wait.

Everyone knew this was a hazard of their job and accepted the risks. This was the first time most of them had experienced it firsthand.

"I'd better call Connie." Trey started to walk toward the locker room to retrieve his phone.

"Give me your keys. I'll head over, let her know what's happening before coming back." Paul had followed Trey.

"Thanks. I want to stay with Jesse. She and Anita are close and I know she'll want to stay until they bring Pete in." He handed Paul his keys. "Stay if Connie's too tired. I'll call you as soon as we find out anything."

"Maybe. I'll see how it is at the house." Paul took off for the parking lot.

Hours later, another officer returned to inform everyone that Lieutenant Baker had been found and was being flown to a hospital an hour away with a trauma unit. At least they knew that Pete was alive.

******

Anita was flown out the same night and landed early the next morning. She went straight to the hospital where she found Jesse, Reb, and Trey sitting in a small waiting room. Jesse ran up to Anita and drew her friend into a hug.

"Come on, I'll go with you to the nurse's station. They won't tell us anything." Anita dropped her flight bag next to Trey as Jesse gripped her friend's hand and led her down the hall. 'This is Mrs. Baker," Jesse told the duty nurse.

"How is he doing? May I see him?" Anita's voice wavered only a little.

"Let me check with the doctor. Go ahead and have a seat. I'll be right back with you, Mrs. Baker."

Not long afterwards Anita was shown into Pete's room, leaving the others with a promise that she'd let them know how he was doing.

Almost an hour went by before Anita came out, her eyes red and swollen. They all stood. Trey opened his arms and she walked into them.

"He looks just awful," she said as her voice broke. She pulled free and grabbed a tissue out of her pocket. "He has a broken arm, broken ankle, and collapsed lung. The doctor says he's critical but expects him to pull through. They'll know more later today."

"Sit down before you fall over." Trey guided her to a chair. "Can I get you anything?"

"Maybe coffee in a little bit. Right now I just need to clear my head." Anita settled into the hard seat and rested her head against the wall. "Pete's pretty out of it with the meds they're giving him, but he recognized me. I just couldn't seem to leave the room until a nurse came in and suggested I take a break."

"Come on, Reb, let's grab some coffee. We'll be right back."

Jesse watched as they walked to the elevators and disappeared inside.

"Trey set up a hotel room for you a few blocks away. We drove two cars so that you can have one without renting. Do you need clothes, anything?"

Anita glanced at Jesse. "No, I brought my flight bag. If I need anything more I'll go buy something. I don't know when I'll use the room—I don't want to be too far from Pete, but I'm so glad you thought of it." She closed her eyes and took a deep breath.

Jesse remained silent, understanding that Anita needed some time alone to process all that had happened. She thought of Trey and if she'd be able to handle something like this as well as Anita.

"I'd had dinner with a couple of friends and had just walked in the door as the phone rang." Anita still sat with her head against the wall, her eyes closed. "The commander said they'd already scheduled a plane to fly me out and a driver was on the way. I remember hanging up the phone and not really thinking. I grabbed my bag, stuffed clothes into it, called my neighbors to let them know what had happened, then walked outside and got into the waiting car. It's all a blur after that."

Jesse reached over and grabbed Anita's hand. "I don't know how you do it. Living across the country from Pete and having to face something like this."

Anita opened her eyes and shifted her gaze to Jesse. "It's simple. I love him." She squeezed Jesse's hand, then closed her eyes again.

Chapter Seventeen

Over a week passed before Pete was moved from critical to stable condition and transported to the hospital near the base. Anita had taken a leave of absence and moved into the house Pete shared with a fellow pilot. She'd come to terms with the accident, Pete's injuries, and the knowledge that changes might be inevitable. She'd told Jesse that you had to learn to adapt to what was thrown your way.

Jesse had seen Trey every day, spent evenings at his house, and gotten to know Trevor better with each visit. She'd already fallen in love with the active toddler and had accepted the fact that marrying Trey was a package deal.

Anita's words kept playing through her mind. Her friend had been able to ease Jesse's fears by the use of five words—*It's simple. I love him.* What had seemed so complex had become quite straightforward. If Jesse truly loved Trey, her answer to him should be simple.

"Good morning, Paul." She walked up beside her squadron mate and took a better look at him. "You look exhausted. Everything all right?"

"Yeah, fine." His grumbled response confirmed for Jesse that something was up.

"I see."

"What does that mean?"

"Not much, except that something is eating at you. You don't have to tell me, just don't say you're fine when you're not. I fly with you, remember? I need to know you're one-hundred percent up there."

Paul came to a halt, pulled off his sunglasses, and glared at Jesse. "It's Connie, all right? She's been gone over a week and yet the lady keeps messing with my mind." He looked up at the clear sky and took a breath. "It will not impact my flying. You got that?"

"Sure, Growler. Loud and clear." Jesse gave him a playful punch on the arm and continued the trek to her plane. She'd been so caught up in her feelings for Trey, and Pete's accident, that a relationship developing between Paul and Connie hadn't been on her radar—now it was.

They flew without incident, ending their day by mid-afternoon and finishing the squadron meeting early. She needed to run a few errands before meeting Anita at the hospital then going to Trey's for dinner.

"How's he doing?" Jesse took a seat next to Anita in Pete's room. He was out. The cuts and bruising on his face had begun to heal, and his breathing had improved as his lung healed. All in all, he was an extremely lucky man.

"Much better. He just drifted off a few minutes ago."

"You have time for coffee?"

"That would be great. I need to get out of this room for a while." Anita grabbed a tote and followed Jesse to the elevators. She leaned against the back wall as they descended to the floor with the cafeteria. "The doctor won't be back for another couple of hours. Honestly, I don't know how Pete gets any sleep with all the activity—it's no wonder they have to give him a sleeping pill to knock him out at night."

They grabbed coffee and took a seat near a window.

"Tell me what's going on with you and Trey. Pete had told me the two of you had split a few months ago."

"About three months ago when he learned about Trevor. My fault—I was an idiot. I left before Trey even brought his son home. I'm sure he thought I'd abandoned him. Maybe I had." Jesse took a sip of coffee and looked over the rim of her cup at Anita. "We're trying to work through it. He's ready to make it permanent, get married, and raise Trevor."

"What do *you* want?" Anita was grateful to be talking about something besides Pete's accident.

"Trey. I just want Trey. You know about my family, how my mother left, and my father and grandmama raised me. I guess watching my father's relationships fall apart, year after year, had a greater impact on me than I knew."

"Don't beat yourself up over it. We're all a product of our upbringing—it's how we choose to deal with it as adults that matters. Sounds like you've come a long way."

"Maybe. Trey wants me to marry him. He needs an answer soon." She blew out a breath, placed her arms on the table, and leaned toward

Anita. "I need the bare truth from you. How is it working, and would you marry Pete again, knowing you'd live apart much of the time?"

There wasn't an instant of hesitation. "In a heartbeat. It's not easy living apart and commuting across the country every few weeks to be together. The alternative is a life without each other, and that's not acceptable to either of us. Can you honestly say your life would be better off without Trey in order to make things less complicated? I know that may sound simplistic, but in a way, love is pretty uncomplicated. We're in this world once, Jesse. Who do you choose to be your partner during the journey?"

******

An hour later Jesse was still mulling over Anita's words as she drove to Trey's. She loved to fly, excelled at it, and was still considering it as a permanent career after her flying obligation was over. At the same time, she knew having a family was important to her. The one person she'd want to build that family with was Trey, and he was willing to do whatever was needed to make it work. He was the strongest and most loyal man she'd ever known. If he said it, he meant it. And she loved him.

Her hands shook as she grabbed the small bag she'd thrown in the back seat.

They'd decided not to complicate things further until Jesse was certain, and sleeping together would make it more difficult for each of them if it didn't work out. She knew by walking in with the bag he'd know she'd made her decision. It was her way of making a final commitment.

"Trey, I'm here," Jesse called as she walked through the door and dropped her black overnight bag on the floor next to the entry table.

"In the kitchen," he called back, and pulled her close when she stopped next to him to inhale the smell of the sauce he had simmering. He leaned down and planted a kiss on her mouth, then a second one. "How are they doing?"

"Pete's improving. He was sleeping when I got there, so I took Anita to the cafeteria. She's a rock."

"That she is." Trey walked to a cupboard and pulled down four plates, then handed them to Jesse. "I heard she applied for a transfer. Is that right?"

Jesse set the table, then grabbed a cold water from the refrigerator. "Yes. The commander told her there was a good chance it would happen. He's got a couple of pilots coming up on the end of their commitment who've notified him they don't plan to extend their time. Pete's roommate told her he'd be willing to move out if the transfer came through. It may all work out fine."

"Smells good," Reb called as he walked into the kitchen. "How's Pete?" he asked Jesse when he saw her standing next to Trey.

"Doing better. I guess the doctor told her they may be able to release him in another week."

"Hope you saved some food for me," Paul called as he walked in from the garage. "Sorry, I got hung up on a phone call."

"No worries, it's just coming out of the oven," Trey replied.

"Ah, your dad's famous enchilada casserole. I love that stuff." Paul tossed his sunglasses on the table as all eyes moved to the stairs at the sound of Trevor's voice. "I'll get him." Paul dashed up the stairs and was back down in five minutes. He placed Trevor in the high chair before grabbing an energy drink. "Man that smells good."

It didn't take the group long to devour the food. Reb had plans with Shelly, and Paul took off to meet some friends for a softball game, leaving Jesse and Trey alone with Trevor.

"You want to watch a movie?" Trey asked as Trevor ran around the living room, grabbing a toy, then discarding it in favor of another one.

"That might be good." Jesse smiled. Trey hadn't noticed what she'd left by the front door.

"You pick one while I grab something from upstairs."

She accessed a movie channel and started reading through the titles while Trevor played with a toy that played music and talked. She clicked on an animated action movie they'd already seen a couple of times, knowing that the movie would be history as soon as Trey discovered the bag.

He walked back into the living room and sat down next to Jesse on the sofa, settling an arm around her shoulders and pulling her toward him. Trevor nuzzled her neck, placing kisses down the soft column, then taking her mouth with his. He moved his lips over hers leisurely, brushing lightly before deepening the kiss. The affect he had on her was always immediate and devastating. His kisses became more ardent, heat creeping through her body, causing Jesse to tighten her hold on his arm until they were interrupted by Trevor tugging on Trey's legs.

"Dada."

Trey pulled away to glance at his son, who rubbed his eyes and laid his head on his father's thigh. Trey picked him up and settled him in his lap. "Looks like we have a tired boy on our hands. He didn't take a nap all day and wasn't down long before dinner. Guess I'll get him to bed."

It didn't take Trey long to get Trevor in bed or for his son to fall asleep. His good fortune. Trey planned to spend as much time alone with Jesse tonight as possible. He wanted an answer, wanted her in his life and in his bed on a permanent basis. The waiting was torture.

Trey sat back down and wrapped Jesse in his arms. It didn't take long to get back to where they were before Trey had taken Trevor upstairs. Within moments, the heat had built to an almost unbearable level. Jesse pulled back and looked up at Trey with glazed eyes.

"I, um, there's something I need. It's by the door. Do you mind getting it?"

He cocked a brow at her but nodded.

Trey stood and walked toward the door. He saw nothing at first, then his eyes locked on the black bag Jesse used for overnight stays. Trey's hand trembled as he reached down to grab the bag.

Jesse saw the bag in Trey's hand before her eyes moved up to lock on his. He placed it on the sofa beside her, then got down on one knee and took her hands.

"Does this mean what I think it does?" His voice was level, smooth, yet a hint of anxious anticipation laced his words.

She smiled, a full smile that was like a punch to Trey's gut.

"Yes."

Trey pulled her to him and wrapped his arms around her, tightening his hold before capturing her mouth with his. He moved his hands to cup her face, placing kisses on her forehead, eyes, and across her face before taking her mouth again for a kiss that promised more than he'd ever be able to put into words.

After several moments, he broke contact. He caressed her cheek with one hand while reaching into his pocket with the other.

"I love you, Jesse. Our life won't be easy, we'll have difficult choices, and neither of us will be happy all the time. If that's a life, and a challenge, you're willing to accept, marry me. You won't regret it."

She wrapped her arms around his neck and gazed into his clear blue eyes. "I love you, Trey. I'll accept the challenge and will gladly build a life with you." She kissed him lightly. "Yes, I'll marry you."

Trey reached for her left hand to slide on a beautiful diamond engagement ring. He looked into her eyes to see a pool of tears threaten to break loose. He placed a kiss on each, tasting the salt from her tears, then moved his lips to her mouth to taste the sweetness she offered. He knew their life would be a mix of everything, an adventure every day, and he was ready to take the ride with her.

Epilogue

"Nana, Nana!" Annie turned to see her grandson, Trevor, run toward her, carrying a small ball in his hand. He reached his arms up and she scooped him up.

"What do you have there?" Annie asked as she gave him a quick kiss on his cheek.

"Ball."

"Yes, it is. Do you know the color?"

"Bue."

Annie smiled. "That's right. Blue. Do you want me to throw it to you?"

Trevor nodded and handed the ball to his grandmother who took it, then set him on the ground. "Here you go." Annie tossed the ball gently to Trevor, who stood three feet away. He caught it and screamed, holding up the ball.

"Looks like he's found a playmate," Heath remarked to Trey. They stood with Jace, Cameron, and Eric, watching the celebration unfold.

The wedding had taken place at the church the MacLarens had attended for years. The pastor was the same one who'd married Heath and Annie, as well as Jace and Caroline. Everyone had then returned to the MacLaren ranch to celebrate Trey and Jesse's marriage.

"Be right back," Trey said and walked toward a tall, slender woman who stood alone. "Hello,

Mother. I wasn't sure you'd be able to make it." He gave her a peck on the cheek, then stepped back.

"Of course I'd make it. You're my son aren't you?" She surveyed the crowd. "Looks like he's still hanging out with the cowboys. Guess things never change."

He loved his mother and was glad she'd driven up from Scottsdale for the wedding. Life with her hadn't been easy and he understood why his parents had separated and then divorced.

"What can I say, Mother? Father is and will always be a cowboy. The same as you'll always be a city girl." He looked for Jesse and found her talking with Reb, Shelly, Paul, and Connie. "Did you have a chance to meet Jesse yet?"

"Yes. Lovely girl, even if she does have a job that's only suited for men, just as nursing is for women." She shielded her eyes to the sun.

Trey chuckled. "Mother, you need to get out more. The world is full of female pilots and male nurses. Who knows? Maybe Cassie will end up being the head of a large, multi-national conglomerate?" Trey knew Cassie's true love was ranching, and maybe someday she'd head up MacLaren Enterprises. It wouldn't surprise him a bit.

"Well, of course Cassie would be able to do that. What kind of daughter do you think I raised?"

Trey could see the twinkle in his mother's eyes. Even though they didn't agree on much, he knew he could count on her when needed, just like he could count on his father.

"Trey!" Trey looked over to see Paul motion him over.

"Excuse me, Mother."

Trey watched as Cameron joined Jesse and their roommates. Annie's two other children, Eric and Brooke, walked up also. He marveled at how the family had grown and continued to expand.

Trey wrapped an arm around Jesse, nuzzled her neck, and pulled her close.

"Okay, guys, there'll be time for that later," Reb joked and grabbed Shelly's hand. "Where are you going on your honeymoon?"

"Right here. There's a cabin up in the hills. Perfect for the two of us for a few days. It'll give Jesse a chance to see more of the ranch, meet my friends, and get to know dad and Annie better. No phone, no television. Sounds good, huh?" He looked to Jesse.

"Sounds great." Her eyes sparkled knowing the next few days would be their one chance to be completely alone.

Heath walked up and stood next to Cameron. "So what's this I hear about getting your helicopter license?"

Trey's gaze shifted to Cameron. "Really, man? You've made the leap?"

"Well, I don't know how much of a leap, but yes, I now have licenses to fly helicopters and small planes. Not quite sure why, it's just something I've wanted to do for a while. The trick now is to get in as many flying hours as I can."

Heath clasped Cam's shoulder. "We'll talk more about this before you fly home."

Annie walked up and put an arm around her son's waist. "You'll be the most multi-talented head of IT in San Francisco."

Cameron smiled at his mother. *If she only knew*, he thought, then raised his glass in a toast to the newlyweds.

"Jesse and Trey. None of us were sure if this day would come. Now that it has, we're all mighty glad to be here, celebrating your marriage. May you have many years of love and adventure."

Trey looked at his new bride and knew the toast was true. Their life would be filled with love and adventure. As much of both as God would allow.

About the Author

Shirleen Davies writes romance—historical, contemporary, and romantic suspense. She grew up in Southern California, attended Oregon State University, and has degrees from San Diego State University and the University of Maryland. During the day she provides consulting services to small and mid-sized businesses. But her real passion is writing emotionally charged stories of flawed people who find redemption through love and acceptance. She now lives with her husband in a beautiful town in northern Arizona.

Shirleen began her series, MacLarens of Fire Mountain, with Tougher than the Rest, the story of the oldest brother, Niall MacLaren. Other books in the series include, Faster than the Rest, Harder than the Rest, Stronger than the Rest, and Deadlier than the Rest. Book six, Wilder than the Rest, is due for release in early summer, 2014. Her contemporary romance series, MacLarens of Fire Mountain Contemporary, opened with book one, Second Summer. Book two, Hard Landing, released in April 2014, and Book three, One More day, is scheduled to release in midsummer, 2014. Book one of her newest historical western series, Redemption Mountain, will release in the fall of 2014.

Shirleen loves to hear from her readers.

Write to her at: shirleen@shirleendavies.com
Visit her website: http://www.shirleendavies.com
Comment on her blog:
http://www.shirleendavies.com/blog.html
Facebook Fan Page:
https://www.facebook.com/ShirleenDaviesAuthor
Twitter: http://twitter.com/shirleendavies
Google+: http://www.gplusid.com/shirleendavies
LinkedIn:
    http://www.linkedin.com/in/shirleendaviesaut
    hor

Other Books by Shirleen Davies

http://www.shirleendavies.com/books.htm
l

Tougher than the Rest – Book One
MacLarens of Fire Mountain Historical Western Romance Series

"A passionate, fast-paced story set in the untamed western frontier by an exciting new voice in historical romance."

Niall MacLaren is the oldest of four brothers, and the undisputed leader of the family. A widower, and single father, his focus is on building the MacLaren ranch into the largest and most successful in northern Arizona. He is serious about two things—his responsibility to the family and his future marriage to the wealthy, well-connected widow who will secure his place in the territory's destiny.

Katherine is determined to live the life she's dreamed about. With a job waiting for her in the growing town of Los Angeles, California, the young teacher from Philadelphia begins a journey across the United States with only a couple of trunks and her spinster companion. Life is perfect for this adventurous, beautiful young woman, until an accident throws her into the arms of the one man who can destroy it all.

Fighting his growing attraction and strong desire for the beautiful stranger, Niall is more determined than ever to push emotions aside to focus on his goals of wealth and political gain. But looking into the clear, blue eyes of the woman who could ruin everything, Niall discovers he will have to harden his heart and be tougher than he's ever been in his life...Tougher than the Rest.

Faster than the Rest – Book Two
MacLarens of Fire Mountain Historical Western Romance Series
"Headstrong, brash, confident, and complex, the MacLarens of Fire Mountain will captivate you with strong characters set in the wild and rugged western frontier."

Handsome, ruthless, young U.S. Marshal Jamie MacLaren had lost everything—his parents, his family connections, and his childhood sweetheart—but now he's back in Fire Mountain and ready for another chance. Just as he successfully reconnects with his family and starts to rebuild his life, he gets the unexpected and unwanted assignment of rescuing the woman who broke his heart.

Beautiful, wealthy Victoria Wicklin chose money and power over love, but is now fighting for her life—or is she? Who has she become in the seven years since she left Fire Mountain to take up her life in San Francisco? Is she really as innocent as she says?

Marshal MacLaren struggles to learn the truth and do his job, but the past and present lead him in different directions as his heart and brain wage battle. Is Victoria a victim or a villain? Is life offering him another chance, or just another heartbreak?

As Jamie and Victoria struggle to uncover past secrets and come to grips with their shared passion, another danger arises. A life-altering danger that is out of their control and threatens to destroy any chance for a shared future.

Harder than the Rest – Book Three
MacLarens of Fire Mountain Historical Western Romance Series
"They are men you want on your side. Hard, confident, and loyal, the MacLarens of Fire Mountain will seize your attention from the first page."

Will MacLaren is a hardened, plain-speaking bounty hunter. His life centers on finding men guilty of horrendous crimes and making sure justice is done. There is no place in his world for the carefree attitude he carried years before when a tragic event destroyed his dreams.

Amanda is the daughter of a successful Colorado rancher. Determined and proud, she works hard to prove she is as capable as any man and worthy to be her father's heir. When a stranger arrives, her independent nature collides with the strong pull toward the handsome ranch hand. But is he what he seems and could his secrets endanger her as well as her family?

The last thing Will needs is to feel passion for another woman. But Amanda elicits feelings he thought were long buried. Can Will's desire for her change him? Or will the vengeance he seeks against the one man he wants to destroy—a dangerous opponent without a conscious— continue to control his life?

Stronger than the Rest – Book Four
MacLarens of Fire Mountain Historical Western Romance Series
"Smart, tough, and capable, the MacLarens protect their own no matter the odds. Set against America's rugged frontier, the stories of the men from Fire Mountain are complex, fast-paced, and a must read for anyone who enjoys non-stop action and romance."

Drew MacLaren is focused and strong. He has achieved all of his goals except one—to return to the MacLaren ranch and build the best horse breeding program in the west. His successful career as an attorney is about to give way to his ranching roots when a bullet changes everything.

Tess Taylor is the quiet, serious daughter of a Colorado ranch family with dreams of her own. Her shy nature keeps her from developing friendships outside of her close-knit family until Drew enters her life. Their relationship grows. Then a bullet, meant for another, leaves him paralyzed and determined to distance himself from the one woman he's come to love.

Convinced he is no longer the man Tess needs, Drew focuses on regaining the use of his legs and recapturing a life he thought lost. But danger of another kind threatens those he cares about—including Tess—forcing him to rethink his future.

Can Drew overcome the barriers that stand between him, the safety of his friends and family, and a life with the woman he loves? To do it all, he has to be strong. Stronger than the Rest.

Deadlier than the Rest – Book Five
MacLarens of Fire Mountain Historical Western Romance Series
"A passionate, heartwarming story of the iconic MacLarens of Fire Mountain. This captivating historical western romance grabs your attention from the start with an engrossing story encompassing two romances set against the rugged backdrop of the burgeoning western frontier."
Connor MacLaren's search has already stolen eight years of his life. Now he is close to finding what he

seeks—Meggie, his missing sister. His quest leads him to the growing city of Salt Lake and an encounter with the most captivating woman he has ever met.

Grace is the third wife of a Mormon farmer, forced into a life far different from what she'd have chosen. Her independent spirit longs for choices governed only by her own heart and mind. To achieve her dreams, she must hide behind secrets and half-truths, even as her heart pulls her towards the ruggedly handsome Connor.

Known as cool and uncompromising, Connor MacLaren lives by a few, firm rules that have served him well and kept him alive. However, danger stalks Connor, even to the front range of the beautiful Wasatch Mountains, threatening those he cares about and impacting his ability to find his sister.

Can Connor protect himself from those who seek his death? Will his eight-year search lead him to his sister while unlocking the secrets he knows are held tight within Grace, the woman who has captured his heart?

Read this heartening story of duty, honor, passion, and love in book five of the MacLarens of Fire Mountain series.

Wilder than the Rest – Book Six

MacLarens of Fire Mountain Historical Western Romance Series

"A captivating historical western romance set in the burgeoning and treacherous city of San Francisco. Go along for the ride in this gripping story that seizes your attention from the very first page."

"If you're a reader who wants to discover an entire family of characters you can fall in love with, this is the series for you." –
Authors to Watch

Pierce is a rough man, but happy in his new life as a Special Agent. Tasked with defending the rights of the federal government, Pierce is a cunning gunslinger always ready to tackle the next job. That is, until he finds out that his new job involves Mollie Jamison.

Mollie can be a lot to handle. Headstrong and independent, Mollie has chosen a life of danger and intrigue guaranteed to prove her liquor-loving father wrong. She will make something of herself, and no one, not even arrogant Pierce MacLaren, will stand in her way.

A secret mission brings them together, but will their attraction to each other prove deadly in their hunt for justice? The payoff for success is high, much higher than any assignment either has taken before. But will the damage to their hearts and souls be too much to bear? Can Pierce and Mollie find a way to overcome their misgivings and work together as one?

Second Summer – Book One
MacLarens of Fire Mountain Contemporary Romance Series

"In this passionate Contemporary Romance, author Shirleen Davies introduces her readers to the modern day MacLarens starting with Heath MacLaren, the head of the family."

The Chairman of both the MacLaren Cattle Co. and MacLaren Land Development, Heath MacLaren is a success professionally—his personal life is another matter.

Following a divorce after a long, loveless marriage, Heath spends his time with women who are beautiful and passionate, yet unable to provide what he longs for . . .

Heath has never experienced love even though he witnesses it every day between his younger brother, Jace, and wife, Caroline. He wants what they have, yet spends his time with women too young to understand what drives him and too focused on themselves to be true companions.

It's been two years since Annie's husband died, leaving her to build a new life. He was her soul mate and confidante. She has no desire to find a replacement, yet longs for male friendship.

Annie's closest friend in Fire Mountain, Caroline MacLaren, is determined to see Annie come out of her shell after almost two years of mourning. A chance meeting with Heath turns into an offer to be a part of the MacLaren Foundation Board and an opportunity for a life outside her home sanctuary which has also become her prison. The platonic friendship that builds between Annie and Heath points to a future where each may rely on the other without the bonds a romance would entail.

However, without consciously seeking it, each yearns for more . . .

The MacLaren Development Company is booming with Heath at the helm. His meetings at a partner company with the young, beautiful marketing director, who makes no secret of her desire for him, are a temptation. But is she the type of woman he truly wants?

Annie's acceptance of the deep, yet passionless, friendship with Heath sustains her, lulling her to believe it is all she needs. At least until Heath drops a bombshell, forcing Annie to realize that what she took for friendship is actually a deep, lasting love. One she doesn't want to lose.

Each must decide to settle—or fight for it all.

Hard Landing – Book Two
MacLarens of Fire Mountain Contemporary Romance Series

Trey MacLaren is a confident, poised Navy pilot. He's focused, loyal, ethical, and a natural leader. He is also on his way to what he hopes will be a lasting relationship and marriage with fellow pilot, Jesse Evans.

Jesse has always been driven. Her graduation from the Naval Academy and acceptance into the pilot training program are all she thought she wanted—until she discovered love with Trey MacLaren

Trey and Jesse's lives are filled with fast flying, friends, and the demands of their military careers. Lives each has settled into with a passion. At least until the day Trey receives a letter that could change his and Jesse's lives forever.

It's been over two years since Trey has seen the woman in Pensacola. Her unexpected letter stuns him and pushes Jesse into a tailspin from which she might not pull back.

Each must make a choice. Will the choice Trey makes cause him to lose Jesse forever? Will she follow her heart or her head as she fights for a chance to save the love she's found? Will their independent decisions collide, forcing them to give up on a life together?

One More Day – Book Three

MacLarens of Fire Mountain Contemporary Romance Series

Cameron "Cam" Sinclair is smart, driven, and dedicated, with an easygoing temperament that belies his strong will and the personal ambitions he holds close. Besides his family, his job as head of IT at the MacLaren Cattle Company and his position as a Search and Rescue volunteer are all he needs to make him happy. At least that's what he thinks until he meets, and is instantly drawn to, fellow SAR volunteer, Lainey Devlin.

Lainey is compassionate, independent, and ready to break away from her manipulative and controlling fiancé. Just as her decision is made, she's called into a major search and rescue effort, where once again, her path crosses with the intriguing, and much too handsome, Cam Sinclair. But Lainey's plans are set. An opportunity to buy a flourishing preschool in northern Arizona is her chance to make a fresh start, and nothing, not even her fierce attraction to Cam Sinclair, will impede her plans.

As Lainey begins to settle into her new life, an unexpected danger arises —threats from an unknown assailant—someone who doesn't believe she belongs in Fire Mountain. The more Lainey begins to love her new home, the greater the danger becomes. Can she accept the help and protection Cam offers while ignoring her consuming desire for him?

Even if Lainey accepts her attraction to Cam, will he ever be able to come to terms with his own driving ambition and allow himself to consider a different life than the one he's always pictured? A life with the one woman who offers more than he'd ever hoped to find?

All Your Nights – Book Four
MacLarens of Fire Mountain Contemporary Romance Series
"Romance, adventure, cowboys, suspense—everything you want in a contemporary western romance novel."

Kade Taylor likes living on the edge. As an undercover agent for the DEA and a former Special Ops team member, his current assignment seems tame—keep tabs on a bookish Ph.D. candidate the agency believes is connected to a ruthless drug cartel.

Brooke Sinclair is weeks away from obtaining her goal of a doctoral degree. She spends time finalizing her presentation and relaxing with another student who seems to want nothing more than her friendship. That's fine with Brooke. Her last serious relationship ended in a broken engagement.

Her future is set, safe and peaceful, just as she's always planned—until Agent Taylor informs her she's under suspicion for illegal drug activities.

Kade and his DEA team obtain evidence which exonerates Brooke while placing her in danger from those who sought to use her. As Kade races to take down the drug cartel while protecting Brooke, he must also find common ground with the former suspect—a woman he desires with increasing intensity.

At odds with her better judgment, Brooke finds the more time she spends with Kade, the more she's attracted to the complex, multi-faceted agent. But Kade holds secrets he knows Brooke will never understand or accept.

Can Kade keep Brooke safe while coming to terms with his past, or will he stay silent, ruining any future with the woman his heart can't let go?

Always Love You– Book Five
MacLarens of Fire Mountain Contemporary Romance Series
"Romance, adventure, motorcycles, cowboys, suspense—everything you want in a contemporary western romance novel."
Eric Sinclair loves his bachelor status. His work at MacLaren Enterprises leaves him with plenty of time to ride his horse as well as his Harley...and

date beautiful women without a thought to commitment.

Amber Anderson is the new person at MacLaren Enterprises. Her passion for marketing landed her what she believes to be the perfect job—until she steps into her first meeting to find the man she left, but still loves, sitting at the management table—his disdain for her clear.

Eric won't allow the past to taint his professional behavior, nor will he repeat his mistakes with Amber, even though love for her pulses through him as strong as ever.

As they strive to mold a working relationship, unexpected danger confronts those close to them, pitting the MacLarens and Sinclairs against an evil who stalks one member but threatens them all.

Eric can't get the memories of their passionate past out of his mind, while Amber wrestles with feelings she thought long buried. Will they be able to put the past behind them to reclaim the love lost years before?

Hearts Don't Lie– Book Six
MacLarens of Fire Mountain Contemporary Romance Series

Mitch MacLaren has reasons for avoiding relationships, and in his opinion, they're pretty darn good. As the new president of RTC Bucking Bulls, difficult challenges occur daily. He certainly doesn't need another one in the form of a fiery, blue-eyed, redhead.

Dana Ballard's new job forces her to work with the one MacLaren who can't seem to get over himself and lighten up. Their verbal sparring is second nature and entertaining until the night of Mitch's departure when he surprises her with a dare she doesn't refuse.

With his assignment in Fire Mountain over, Mitch is free to return to Montana and run the business his father helped start. The glitch in his enthusiasm has to do with one irreversible mistake—the dare Dana didn't ignore. Now, for reasons that confound him, he just can't let it go.

Working together is a circumstance neither wants, but both must accept. As their attraction grows, so do the accidents and strange illnesses of the animals RTC depends on to stay in business. Mitch's total focus should be on finding the reasons and people behind the incidents. Instead, he finds himself torn between his unwanted desire for Dana and the business which is his life.

In his mind, a simple proposition can solve one problem. Will Dana make the smart move and walk away? Or take the gamble and expose her heart?

No Getting Over You– Book Seven
MacLarens of Fire Mountain Contemporary Romance Series

Cassie MacLaren has come a long way since being dumped by her long-time boyfriend, a man she believed to be her future. Successful in her job at MacLaren Enterprises, dreaming of one day leading one of the divisions, she's moved on to start a new relationship, having little time to dwell on past mistakes.

Matt Garner loves his job as rodeo representative for Double Ace Bucking Stock. Busy days and constant travel leave no time for anything more than the occasional short-term relationship— which is just the way he likes it. He's come to accept the regret of leaving the woman he loved for the pro rodeo circuit.

The future is set for both, until a chance meeting ignites long buried emotions neither is willing to face.

Forced to work together, their attraction grows, even as multiple arson fires threaten Cassie's new home of Cold Creek, Colorado. Although Cassie believes the danger from the fires is remote, she knows the danger Matt poses to her heart is real.

While fighting his renewed feelings for Cassie, Matt focuses on a new and unexpected opportunity offered by MacLaren Enterprises—an opportunity that will put him on a direct collision course with Cassie.

Will pride and self-preservation control their future? Or will one be strong enough to make the first move, risking everything, including their heart?

Redemption's Edge – Book One
Redemption Mountain – Historical Western Romance Series
"A heartwarming, passionate story of loss, forgiveness, and redemption set in the untamed frontier during the tumultuous years following the Civil War. Ms. Davies' engaging and complex characters draw you in from the start, creating an exciting introduction to this new historical western romance series."

"Redemption's Edge is a strong and engaging introduction to her new historical western romance series."

Dax Pelletier is ready for a new life, far away from the one he left behind in Savannah following the South's devastating defeat in the Civil War. The ex-Confederate general wants nothing more to do with commanding men and confronting the tough truths of leadership.

Rachel Davenport possesses skills unlike those of her Boston socialite peers—skills honed as a nurse in field hospitals during the Civil War. Eschewing her northeastern suitors and changed by the carnage she's seen, Rachel decides to accept her uncle's invitation to assist him at his clinic in the dangerous and wild frontier of Montana.

Now a Texas Ranger, a promise to a friend takes Dax and his brother, Luke, to the untamed territory of Montana. He'll fulfill his oath and return to Austin, at least that's what he believes.

The small town of Splendor is what Rachel needs after life in a large city. In a few short months, she's grown to love the people as well as the majestic beauty of the untamed frontier. She's settled into a life unlike any she has ever thought possible.

Thinking his battle days are over, he now faces dangers of a different kind—one by those from his past who seek vengeance, and another from Rachel, the woman who's captured his heart.

Wildfire Creek – Book Two
Redemption Mountain – Historical Western Romance Series

"A passionate story of rebuilding lives, working to find a place in the wild frontier, and building new lives in the years following the American Civil War. A rugged, heartwarming story of choices and love in the continuing saga of Redemption Mountain."

Luke Pelletier is settling into his new life as a rancher and occasional Pinkerton Agent, leaving his past as an ex-Confederate major and Texas Ranger far behind. He wants nothing more than to work the ranch, charm the ladies, and live a life of carefree bachelorhood.

Ginny Sorensen has accepted her responsibility as the sole provider for herself and her younger sister. The desire to continue their journey to Oregon is crushed when the need for food and shelter keeps them in the growing frontier town of Splendor, Montana, forcing Ginny to accept work as a server in the local saloon.

Luke has never met a woman as lovely and unspoiled as Ginny. He longs to know her, yet fears his wild ways and unsettled nature aren't what she deserves. She's a girl you marry, but that is nowhere in Luke's plans.

Complicating their tenuous friendship, a twist in circumstances forces Ginny closer to the man she most wants to avoid—the man who can destroy her dreams, and who's captured her heart.

Believing his bachelor status firm, Luke moves from danger to adventure, never dreaming each step he takes brings him closer to his true destiny and a life much different from what he imagines.

Sunrise Ridge – Book Three
Redemption Mountain – Historical Western Romance Series
"The author has a talent for bringing the historical west to life, realistically and vividly, and doesn't shy away from some of the harder aspects of frontier life, even though it's fiction. Recommended to readers who like sweeping western historical romances that are grounded with memorable, likeable characters and a strong sense of place."

Noah Brandt is a successful blacksmith and businessman in Splendor, Montana, with few ties to his past as an ex-Union Army major and sharpshooter. Quiet and hardworking, his biggest challenge is controlling his strong desire for a woman he believes is beyond his reach.

Abigail Tolbert is tired of being under her father's thumb while at the same time, being pushed away by the one man she desires. Determined to build a new life outside the control of her wealthy father, she finds work and sets out to shape a life on her own terms.

Noah has made too many mistakes with Abby to have any hope of getting her back. Even with the changes in her life, including the distance she's built with her father, he can't keep himself from believing he'll never be good enough to claim her.

Unexpected dangers, including a twist of fate for Abby, change both their lives, making the tentative steps they've taken to build a relationship a distant hope. As Noah battles his past as well as the threats to Abby, she fights for a future with the only man she will ever love.

Dixie Moon – Book Four
Redemption Mountain – Historical Western Romance Series

Gabe Evans is a man of his word with strong convictions and steadfast loyalty. As the sheriff of Splendor, Montana, the ex-Union Colonel and oldest of four boys from an affluent family, Gabe understands the meaning of responsibility. The last thing he wants is another commitment—especially of the female variety.

Until he meets Lena Campanel...

Lena's past is one she intends to keep buried. Overcoming a childhood of setbacks and obstacles, she and her friend, Nick, have succeeded in creating a life of financial success and devout loyalty to one another.

When an unexpected death leaves Gabe the sole heir of a considerable estate, partnering with Nick and Lena is a lucrative decision...forcing Gabe and Lena to work together. As their desire grows, Lena refuses to let down her guard, vowing to keep her past hidden—even from a perfect man like Gabe. But secrets never stay buried...

When revealed, Gabe realizes Lena's secrets are deeper than he ever imagined. For a man of his character, deception and lies of omission aren't negotiable. Will he be able to forgive the deceit? Or is the damage too great to ever repair?

Survivor Pass – Book Five
Redemption Mountain – Historical Western Romance Series

He thought he'd found a quiet life...
Cash Coulter settled into a life far removed from his days of fighting for the South and crossing the country as a bounty hunter. Now a deputy sheriff, Cash wants nothing more than to buy some land, raise cattle, and build a simple life in the frontier town of Splendor, Montana. But his whole world shifts when his gaze lands on the most captivating woman he's ever seen. And the feeling appears to be mutual.

But nothing is as it seems...
Alison McGrath moved from her home in Kentucky to the rugged mountains of Montana for one reason—to find the man responsible for murdering her brother. Despite using a false identity to avoid any tie to her brother's name, the citizens of Splendor have no intention of sharing their knowledge about the bank robbery which killed her only sibling. Alison knows her circle of lies can't end well, and her growing for Cash threatens to weaken the revenge which drives her.

And the troubles are mounting...
There is danger surrounding them both—men who seek vengeance as a way to silence the past...by any means necessary.

Reclaiming Love – Book One, A Novella

Peregrine Bay – Contemporary Romance Series

Adam Monroe has seen his share of setbacks. Now he's back in Peregrine Bay, looking for a new life and second chance.

Julia Kerrigan's life rebounded after the sudden betrayal of the one man she ever loved. As president of a success real estate company, she's built a new life and future, pushing the painful past behind her.

Adam's reason for accepting the job as the town's new Police Chief can be explained in one word—Julia. He wants her back and will do whatever is necessary to achieve his goal, even knowing his biggest hurdle is the woman he still loves.

As they begin to reconnect, a terrible scandal breaks loose with Julia and Adam at the center. Will the threat to their lives and reputations destroy their fledgling romance? Can Adam identify and eliminate the danger to Julia before he's had a chance to reclaim her love?

Our Kind of Love – Book Two

Peregrine Bay – Contemporary Romance Series

Selena Kerrigan is content with a life filled with work and family, never feeling the need to take a chance on a relationship—until she steps into a social world inhabited by a man with dark hair and penetrating blue eyes. Eyes that are fixed on her.

Lincoln Caldwell is a man satisfied with his life. Transitioning from an enviable career as a Navy SEAL to becoming a successful entrepreneur, his days focus on growing his security firm, spending his nights with whomever he chooses. Committing to one woman isn't on the horizon—until a captivating woman with caramel eyes sends his personal life into a tailspin.

Believing her identity remains a secret, Selena returns to work, ready to forget about running away from the bed she never should have gone near. She's prepared to put the colossal error, as well as the man she'll never see again, behind her.

Too bad the object of her lapse in judgment doesn't feel the same.

Linc is good at tracking his targets, and Selena is now at the top of his list. It's amazing how a pair of sandals and only a first name can say so much.

As he pursues the woman he can't rid from his mind, a series of cyber-attacks hit his business, threatening its hard-won success. Worse, and unbeknownst to most, Linc harbors a secret—one with the potential to alter his life, along with those he's close to, in ways he could never imagine.

Our Kind of Love, Book Two in the Peregrine Bay Contemporary Romance series, is a full-length novel with an HEA and no cliffhanger.

Colin's Quest – Book One
MacLarens of Boundary Mountain – Historical Western Romance Series
For An Undying Love...
When Colin MacLaren headed west on a wagon train, he hoped to find adventure and perhaps a little danger in untamed California. He never expected to meet the girl he would love forever. He also never expected her to be the daughter of his family's age-old enemy, but Sarah was a MacGregor and the anger he anticipated soon became a reality. Her father would not be swayed, vehemently refusing to allow marriage to a MacLaren.

Time Has No Effect...
Forced apart for five years, Sarah never forgot Colin—nor did she give up on his promise to come for her. Carrying the brooch he gave her as proof of their secret betrothal, she scans the trail from California, waiting for Colin to claim her. Unfortunately, her father has other plans.

And Enemies Hold No Power.
Nothing can stop Colin from locating Sarah. Not outlaws, runaways, or miles of difficult trails.

However, reuniting is only the beginning. Together they must find the courage to fight the men who would keep them apart—and conquer the challenge of uniting two independent hearts.

Find all of my books at:
http://www.shirleendavies.com/books.html

For permission requests, contact the publisher.
Avalanche Ranch Press, LLC
PO Box 12618
Prescott, AZ 86304

Made in the USA
Coppell, TX
14 September 2020